P9-BYE-310

THE STORY OF SYLVIE AND BRUNO

by Lewis Carroll
illustrated by Harry Furniss

being a facsimile edition published by

MAYFLOWER BOOKS · NEW YORK

in association with

Macmillan · London

Facsimile Classics Series

ENGLISH FAIRY TALES
by Flora Annie Steel
illustrated by Arthur Rackham

THE WATER-BABIES
by Charles Kingsley
illustrated by Linley Sambourne and J. MacFarlane

THE HEROES OF ASGARD
by A. and E. Keary
illustrated by Charles E. Brock

THE MIKADO
by Sir W. S. Gilbert
illustrated by W. Russell Flint and Charles E. Brock

THE FABLES OF AESOP
edited by Joseph Jacobs
illustrated by Richard Heighway

THE ROMANCE OF KING ARTHUR
by Alfred W. Pollard abridged from Malory
illustrated by Arthur Rackham

OLD CHRISTMAS
by Washington Irving
illustrated by Randolph Caldecott

GRIMM'S HOUSEHOLD STORIES
translated by Lucy Crane
illustrated by Walter Crane

THE FAIRY BOOK
by Dinah Maria Mulock
illustrated by Warwick Goble

JAPANESE FAIRY TALES
by Grace James
illustrated by Warwick Goble

THE NURSERY 'ALICE'
by Lewis Carroll
illustrated by Sir John Tenniel

THE YEOMEN OF THE GUARD
by Sir W. S. Gilbert
illustrated by W. Russell Flint and Charles E. Brock

THE CUCKOO CLOCK
by Mary Louisa Molesworth
illustrated by Charles E. Brock

THE STORY OF SYLVIE AND BRUNO
by Lewis Carroll
illustrated by Harry Furniss

THE HEROES
by Charles Kingsley
illustrated by H. M. Brock

JUST SO STORIES
by Rudyard Kipling
illustrated by the author and Joseph M. Gleeson

RIP VAN WINKLE and THE LEGEND OF SLEEPY HOLLOW
by Washington Irving
illustrated by George H. Boughton

THE STORY OF SYLVIE AND BRUNO

BY

LEWIS CARROLL

WITH ILLUSTRATIONS BY HARRY FURNISS

MACMILLAN AND CO., LIMITED
ST. MARTIN'S STREET, LONDON
1926

First published by Macmillan & Co. 1904
First published in this edition 1980 by
MAYFLOWER BOOKS INC.
575 Lexington Avenue New York City 10022

Library of Congress Cataloging in Publication Data
Dodgson, Charles Lutwidge, 1832-1898.
The story of Sylvie and Bruno.

(Facsimile classics series)
"Culled from the two volumes of Sylvie and Bruno."
Photoreprint of the 1926 issue of the work originally published in 1904 by Macmillan, London.
SUMMARY: Selected portions from "Sylvie and Bruno" in which two fairy children meet adventure in such places as Dogland, Outland, and Elfland.
[1. Fantasy] I. Title. II. Series.
PZ7.D684St 1980 [Fic] 79-22513
ISBN 0-8317-8602-7

Printed in Hong Kong

SWAIN SC

PREFACE

THIS book, culled from the two volumes of *Sylvie and Bruno*, contains only the portions about the two fairy children (with the original illustrations) in the words of Lewis Carroll, without any extraneous matter. A few words only have in some places been added or altered, when *absolutely necessary* to dovetail the different paragraphs together, so as to make the "Story" one consecutive whole. The humour in this book is so unique and fascinating, that *The Story of Sylvie and Bruno* is likely in this form to become as popular as the *Alice* books by the same author.

Thou delicious Fay—
The guardian of a Sprite that lives to tease thee—
Loving in earnest, chiding but in play
The merry mocking Bruno! Who, that sees thee,
Can fail to love thee, Darling, even as I?—
My sweetest Sylvie, we must say 'Good-bye!'

CONTENTS

THE STORY OF SYLVIE AND BRUNO

CHAPTER I

THE PROFESSOR

THE Warden, a tall dignified man with a grave but very pleasant face, was seated before a writing-table, which was covered with papers, and holding on his knee one of the sweetest and loveliest little maidens it has ever been my lot to see. She looked four or five years older than Bruno, but she had the same rosy cheeks and sparkling eyes, and the same wealth of curly brown hair. Her eager smiling face was turned upwards towards her father's, and it was a pretty sight to see the mutual love with which the two faces—one in the Spring of Life, the other in its late Autumn—were gazing on each other.

"No, you've never seen him," the old man was saying: "you couldn't, you know, he's been away so long—travelling from land to land, and seeking for health, more years than you've been alive, little Sylvie!"

Here Bruno climbed upon his other knee, and a good deal of kissing, on a rather complicated system, was the result.

"He only came back last night," said the Warden, when the kissing was over: "he's been traveling post-haste, for the last thousand miles or so, in order to be here on Sylvie's birthday. But he's a very early riser, and I dare say he's in the Library already. Come with me and see him. He's always kind to children. You'll be sure to like him."

"Has the Other Professor come too?" Bruno asked in an awe-struck voice.

"Yes, they arrived together. The Other Professor is—well, you won't like him quite so much, perhaps. He's a little more *dreamy*, you know."

"I wiss *Sylvie* was a little more dreamy," said Bruno.

"What *do* you mean, Bruno?" said Sylvie.

Bruno went on addressing his father. "She says she *ca'n't*, oo know. But I thinks it isn't *ca'n't*, it's *wo'n't*."

"Says she *ca'n't* dream!" the puzzled Warden repeated.

"She *do* say it," Bruno persisted. "When I says to her, 'Let's stop lessons!', she says, 'Oh, I ca'n't *dream* of letting oo stop yet!'"

"He always wants to stop lessons," Sylvie explained, "five minutes after we begin!"

"Five minutes' lessons a day," said the Warden. "You won't learn much at *that* rate, little man!"

"That's just what Sylvie says," Bruno rejoined. "She says I *wo'n't* learn my lessons. And I tells her, over and over, I *ca'n't* learn 'em. And what doos oo think she says? She says 'It isn't *ca'n't*, it's *wo'n't!*'"

"Let's go and see the Professor," the Warden said, wisely avoiding further discussion. The children got down off his knees, each secured a hand, and the happy trio set off for the Library—followed by me. I had come to the conclusion by this time that none of the party was in the least able to see me.

"What's the matter with him?" Sylvie asked, walking with a little extra sedateness, by way of example to Bruno at the other side, who never ceased jumping up and down.

"What *was* the matter—but I hope he's all right now—was lumbago, and rheumatism, and that kind of thing. He's been curing *himself*, you know: he's a very learned doctor. Why, he's actually *invented* three new diseases, besides a new way of breaking your collar-bone!"

"Is it a nice way?" said Bruno.

"Well, hum, not *very*," the Warden said, as we entered the Library. "And here *is* the Professor. Good morning, Professor! Hope you're quite rested after your journey!"

A jolly-looking, fat little man, in a flowery dressing-gown, with a large book under each arm, came trotting in at the other end of the room, and was going straight across without taking any notice of the children. "I'm looking for Vol. Three," he said. "Do you happen to have seen it?"

"You don't see my *children*, Professor!" the Warden exclaimed, taking him by the shoulders and turning him round to face them.

The Professor laughed violently: then he gazed at them through his great spectacles, for a minute or two, without speaking.

At last he addressed Bruno. "I hope you have had a good night, my child?"

Bruno looked puzzled. "I's had the same night *oo've* had," he replied. "There's only been *one* night since yesterday!"

It was the Professor's turn to look puzzled now. He took off his spectacles, and rubbed them with his handkerchief. Then he gazed at them again. Then he turned to the Warden. "Are they bound?" he enquired.

"No, we aren't," said Bruno, who thought himself quite able to answer *this* question.

The Professor shook his head sadly. "Not even half-bound?"

"Why *would* we be half-bound?" said Bruno. "We're not prisoners!"

But the Professor had forgotten all about them by this time, and was speaking to the Warden again. "You'll be glad to hear," he was saying, "that the Barometer's beginning to move——"

"Well, which way?" said the Warden—adding to the children, "Not that *I* care, you know. Only *he* thinks it affects the weather. He's a wonderfully clever man, you know. Sometimes he says things that only the Other Professor can understand. Sometimes he says things that *nobody* can understand! Which way is it, Professor? Up or down?"

"Neither!" said the Professor, gently clapping his hands. "It's going sideways—if I may so express myself."

"And what kind of weather does *that* produce?" said the Warden. "Listen, children! Now you'll hear something worth knowing!"

"Horizontal weather," said the Professor, and made straight for the door, very nearly trampling on Bruno, who had only just time to get out of his way.

"*Isn't* he learned?" the Warden said, looking after him with admiring eyes "Positively he runs over with learning!"

"But he needn't run over *me!*" said Bruno.

The Professor was back in a moment: he had changed his dressing-gown for a frock-coat, and had put on a pair of very strange-looking boots, the tops of which were open umbrellas. "I thought you'd like to see them," he said. "*These* are the boots for horizontal weather!"

"But what's the use of wearing umbrellas round one's knees?"

"In *ordinary* rain," the Professor admitted, "they would *not* be of much use. But if ever it rained *horizontally*, you know, they would be invaluable—simply invaluable!"

"Take the Professor to the breakfast-saloon, children," said the Warden. "And tell them not to wait for me. I had breakfast early, as

I've some business to attend to." The children seized the Professor's hands, as familiarly as if they had known him for years, and hurried him away. I followed respectfully behind.

CHAPTER II

SYLVIE'S BIRTHDAY

As we entered the breakfast-saloon, the Professor was saying "—and he had breakfast by himself, early: so he begged you wouldn't wait for him, my Lady."

"Then there's no use waiting!" said my Lady. "Let's sit down. Uggug, my pet, come and sit by me!"

"Anywhere but by *me!*" growled the Sub-Warden. "The little wretch always manages to upset his coffee!"

I guessed at once (as perhaps the reader will also have guessed, if, like myself, he is *very* clever at drawing conclusions) that my Lady was the Sub-Warden's wife, and that Uggug (a hideous fat boy, about the same age as Sylvie, with the expression of a prize-pig) was their son. Sylvie and Bruno, with the Lord Chancellor, made up a party of seven.

"Excuse me a moment," said the Professor. "As this is Lady Sylvie's birthday, I would like to——" and he rushed away.

Bruno began feeling in his pockets, looking more and more melancholy as he did so: then he put his thumb in his mouth, and considered for a minute: then he quietly left the room.

He had hardly done so before the Professor was back again, quite out of breath. "Wishing you many happy returns of the day, my dear child!" he went on, addressing the smiling little girl, who had run to meet him. "Allow me to give you a birthday-present. It's a second-hand pincushion, my dear. And it only cost fourpence-halfpenny!"

"Thank you, it's *very* pretty!" And Sylvie rewarded the old man with a hearty kiss.

"And the *pins* they gave me for nothing!" the Professor added in high glee. "Fifteen of 'em, and only *one* bent!"

"I'll make the bent one into a *hook!*" said

Sylvie. "To catch Bruno with, when he runs away from his lessons!"

"You ca'n't guess what *my* present is!" said Uggug, who had taken the butter-dish from the table, and was standing behind her, with a wicked leer on his face.

"No, I ca'n't guess," Sylvie said without looking up. She was still examining the Professor's pincushion.

"It's *this!*" cried the bad boy, exultingly, as he emptied the dish over her, and then, with a grin of delight at his own cleverness, looked round for applause.

Sylvie coloured crimson, as she shook off the butter from her frock: but she kept her lips tight shut, and walked away to the window, where she stood looking out and trying to recover her temper.

Uggug's triumph was a very short one: the Sub-Warden had returned, just in time to be a witness of his dear child's playfulness, and in another moment a skilfully-applied box on the ear had changed the grin of delight into a howl of pain.

At this moment Bruno re-entered the room,

and passing Uggug (who was blubbering his loudest, in the hope of attracting notice) as if he was quite used to that sort of thing, he ran up to Sylvie and threw his arms round her. "I went to my toy-cupboard," he said with a very sorrowful face, " to see if there were *somefin* fit for a present for oo! And there isn't *nuffin!* They's *all* broken, every one! And I haven't got *no* money left, to buy oo a birthday-present! And I ca'n't give oo nuffin but *this!*" ("*This*" was a very earnest hug and a kiss.)

"Oh, thank you, darling!" cried Sylvie. "I like *your* present best of all!" (But if so, why did she give it back so quickly?)

His Sub-Excellency turned and patted the two children on the head with his long lean hands. "Go away, dears!" he said. "There's business to talk over."

Sylvie and Bruno went away hand in hand; but, on reaching the door, Sylvie came back again and went up to Uggug timidly. "I don't mind about the butter," she said, "and I—I'm sorry he hurt you!" And she tried to shake hands with the little ruffian: but Uggug only blubbered louder, and wouldn't make friends. Sylvie left the room with a sigh.

The Sub-Warden glared angrily at his weeping son. "Leave the room, Sirrah!" he said. The door opened, and Sylvie and Bruno came in, with their arms twined lovingly round each other—Bruno sobbing convulsively, with his face hidden on his sister's shoulder, and Sylvie more grave and quiet, but with tears streaming down her cheeks.

"Mustn't cry like that!" the Vice-Warden said sharply, but without any effect on the weeping children. "Cheer 'em up a bit!" he hinted to my Lady.

"*Cake!*" my lady muttered to herself with great decision, crossing the room and opening a cupboard, from which she presently returned with two slices of plum cake. "Eat, and don't cry!" were her short and simple orders: and the poor children sat down side by side, but seemed in no mood for eating.

For the second time the door opened—or rather was *burst* open, this time, as Uggug rushed violently into the room, shouting "that old Beggar's come again!"

"He's not to have any food——" the Vice-Warden was beginning, but the Chancellor interrupted him. "It's all right," he said, in a low voice: "the servants have their orders."

"He's just under here," said Uggug, who had gone to the window, and was looking down into the court-yard.

"Where, my darling?" said his fond mother, flinging her arms round the neck of the little monster. All of us (except Sylvie and

Bruno, who took no notice of what was going on) followed her to the window. The old Beggar looked up at us with hungry eyes. "Only a crust of bread, your Highness!" he pleaded. He was a fine old man, but looked sadly ill and worn. "A crust of bread is what I crave!" he repeated. "A single crust, and a little water!"

"Here's some water, drink this!" Uggug bellowed, emptying a jug of water over his head.

"Well done, my boy!" cried the Vice-Warden. "That's the way to settle such folk!"

"Clever boy!" the Wardeness chimed in. "*Hasn't* he good spirits?"

"Take a stick to him!" shouted the Vice-Warden, as the old Beggar shook the water from his ragged cloak, and again gazed meekly upwards.

"Take a red-hot poker to him!" my Lady again chimed in.

Possibly there was no red-hot poker handy: but some *sticks* were forthcoming in a moment, and threatening faces surrounded the poor old wanderer, who waved them back with quiet dignity. "No need to break my old bones," he said. "I am going. Not even a crust!"

"Poor, *poor* old man!" exclaimed a little voice at my side, half choked with sobs. Bruno was at the window, trying to throw out his slice of plum-cake, but Sylvie held him back.

"He *shall* have my cake!" Bruno cried, passionately struggling out of Sylvie's arms.

"Yes, yes, darling!" Sylvie gently pleaded. "But don't *throw* it out! He's gone away, don't you see? Let's go after him." And she led him out of the room, unnoticed by the rest of the party, who were wholly absorbed in watching the old Beggar.

CHAPTER III

ELFLAND

THEN suddenly there sounded

> "*He thought he saw an Elephant,*
> *That practised on a fife:*
> *He looked again, and found it was*
> *A letter from his wife.*
> *'At length I realise,' he said,*
> *'The bitterness of Life!'*"

What a wild being it was who sang these wild words! A Gardener he seemed to be—yet surely a mad one, by the way he brandished his rake—madder, by the way he broke, ever and anon, into a frantic jig—maddest of all, by the

C

shriek in which he brought out the last words of the stanza!

It was so far a description of himself that he had the *feet* of an Elephant: but the rest of him was skin and bone: and the wisps of loose straw, that bristled all about him, suggested that he had been originally stuffed with it, and that nearly all the stuffing had come out.

Sylvie and Bruno waited patiently till the end of the first verse. Then Sylvie advanced alone (Bruno having suddenly turned shy) and timidly introduced herself with the words "Please, I'm Sylvie!"

"And who's that other thing?" said the Gardener.

"What thing?" said Sylvie, looking round. "Oh, that's Bruno. He's my brother."

"Was he your brother yesterday?" the Gardener anxiously enquired.

"Course I were!" cried Bruno, who had gradually crept nearer, and didn't at all like being talked about without having his share in the conversation.

"Ah, well!" the Gardener said with a kind of groan. "Things change so, here. Whenever I look again, it's sure to be something different! Yet I does my duty! I gets up wriggle-early at five——"

"If I was *oo*," said Bruno, "I wouldn't wriggle so early. It's as bad as being a worm!" he added, in an undertone to Sylvie.

"But you shouldn't be lazy in the morning, Bruno," said Sylvie. "Remember, it's the *early* bird that picks up the worm!"

"It may, if it likes!" Bruno said with a slight yawn. "I don't like eating worms, one bit. I always stop in bed till the early bird has picked them up!"

"I wonder you've the face to tell me such fibs!" cried the Gardener.

To which Bruno wisely replied, "Oo don't want a *face* to tell fibs wiz—only a *mouf*."

Sylvie discreetly changed the subject. "And did you plant all these flowers?" she said. "What a lovely garden you've made! Do you know, I'd like to live here *always!*"

"In the winter-nights——" the Gardener was beginning.

"But I'd nearly forgotten what we came about!" Sylvie interrupted. "Would you please let us through into the road? There's a poor old beggar just gone out—and he's very hungry—and Bruno wants to give him his cake, you know!"

"It's as much as my place is worth!" the Gardener muttered, taking a key from his pocket, and beginning to unlock a door in the garden-wall.

"How much *are* it wurf?" Bruno innocently enquired.

But the Gardener only grinned. "That's a secret!" he said. "Mind you come back quick!" he called after the children, as they passed out into the road. I had just time to follow them, before he shut the door again.

We hurried down the road, and very soon caught sight of the old Beggar, about a quarter of a mile ahead of us, and the children at once set off running to overtake him. Lightly and swiftly they skimmed over the ground, and I could not in the least understand how it was I kept up with them so easily.

The old Beggar must have been very deaf, as he paid no attention whatever to Bruno's eager shouting, but trudged wearily on, never pausing until the child got in front of him and held up the slice of cake. The poor little fellow was quite out of breath, and could only utter the one word "Cake!"—not with the gloomy decision with which Her Excellency had so lately pronounced it, but with a sweet childish timidity.

The old man snatched it from him, and devoured it greedily, as some hungry wild beast might have done, but never a word of thanks did he give his little benefactor—only growled "More, more!" and glared at the half-frightened children.

"There *is* no more!" Sylvie said with tears in her eyes. "I'd eaten mine. It was a shame to let you be turned away like that. I'm very sorry——"

I lost the rest of the sentence.

"Follow me!" were the next words I heard, as the old man waved his hand, with a dignified grace that ill suited his ragged dress, over a bush that stood by the road side, which began instantly to sink into the earth.

When the bush had sunk quite out of our sight, marble steps were seen, leading downwards into darkness. The old man led the way, and we eagerly followed.

"We are safe here, my darlings!" said the old man, laying a hand on Sylvie's shoulder, and bending down to kiss her. Sylvie drew back hastily, with an offended air: but in another moment, with a glad cry of "Why, it's *Father!*", she had run into his arms.

"Father! Father!" Bruno repeated: and, while the happy children were being hugged and kissed, I could but rub my eyes and say, "Where, then, are the rags gone to?"; for the old man was now dressed in royal robes that glittered with jewels and gold embroidery, and wore a circlet of gold around his head.

"Where are we, father?" Sylvie whispered, with her arms twined closely around the old man's neck, and with her rosy cheek lovingly pressed to his.

"In Elfland, darling. It's one of the provinces of Fairyland."

"But I thought Elfland was *ever* so far from Outland: and we've come such a *tiny* little way!"

"You came by the Royal Road, sweet one. Only those of royal blood can travel along it: but *you've* been royal ever since I was made King of Elfland—that's nearly a month ago. They sent *two* ambassadors, to make sure that their invitation to me, to be their new King, should reach me. One was a Prince; so *he* was able to come by the Royal Road, and to come invisibly to all but me: the other was a Baron; so *he* had to come by the common road, and I dare say he hasn't even *arrived* yet."

"Then how far have we come?" Sylvie enquired.

"Just a thousand miles, sweet one, since the Gardener unlocked that door for you."

"A thousand miles!" Bruno repeated. "And may I eat one?"

"Eat a *mile*, little rogue?"

"No," said Bruno. "I mean may I eat one of that fruits?"

"Yes, child," said his father.

Bruno ran eagerly to the wall, and picked a fruit that was *shaped* something like a banana, but had the *colour* of a strawberry.

He ate it with beaming looks, that became gradually more gloomy, and were very blank indeed by the time he had finished.

"It hasn't got no taste at all!" he complained. "I couldn't feel nuffin in my mouf! It's a—what's that hard word, Sylvie?"

"It was a *Phlizz*," Sylvie gravely replied. "Are they *all* like that, father?"

"They're all like that to *you*, darling, because you don't belong to Elfland—yet. But to *me* they are real."

Bruno looked puzzled. "I'll try anuvver kind of fruits!" he said, and jumped down off the King's knee. "There's some lovely striped ones, just like a rainbow!" And off he ran.

CHAPTER IV

THE MAD GARDENER

AND then, suddenly and swiftly, the darkness of midnight seemed to close in upon us, and through the darkness harshly rang a strange wild song :—

> "*He thought he saw a Buffalo*
> *Upon the chimney-piece :*
> *He looked again, and found it was*
> *His Sister's Husband's Niece.*

'Unless you leave this house,' he said,
'I'll send for the Police!'"

"That was *me!*" he added, looking out at us, through the half-opened door, as we stood waiting in the road. "And that's what I'd have done—as sure as potatoes aren't radishes —if she hadn't have tooken herself off! But I always loves my *pay-rints* like anything."

"Who *are* oor *pay-rints?*" said Bruno.

"Them as pay *rint* for me, a course!" the Gardener replied. "You can come in now, if you like."

He flung the door open as he spoke, and we went in.

It seemed natural enough that the Gardener should be filled with exuberant delight at the return of so gracious a master and mistress— less natural that he should show it by such wild dances, such crazy songs!

"He thought he saw a Rattlesnake
That questioned him in Greek:
He looked again, and found it was
The Middle of Next Week.
'The one thing I regret,' he said,
'Is that it cannot speak!'"

And once more those shrill discordant tones rang out :—

"*He thought he saw a Banker's Clerk*
Descending from the bus :

He looked again, and found it was
A Hippopotamus :
'If this should stay to dine,' he said,
'There won't be much for us!'"

Throwing away the spade, he broke into a frantic jig, snapping his fingers, and repeating, again and again,

> "*There won't be much for us!*
> *There won't be much for us!*"

The silence that followed was broken by the sweet voice of Sylvie. "Would you please let us out into the road?"

"What! After that old beggar again?" the Gardener yelled, and began singing:—

"*He thought he saw a Kangaroo*
That worked a coffee-mill:

He looked again, and found it was
A Vegetable-Pill.
'Were I to swallow this,' he said,
'I should be very ill!'"

"We don't want him to swallow *anything*," Sylvie explained. "He's not hungry. But we want to see him. So will you please——"

"Certainly!" the Gardener promptly replied. "I *always* please. Never displeases nobody. There you are!" And he flung the door open, and let us out upon the dusty high-road.

CHAPTER V

WAYS AND MEANS

We soon found our way to the bush, which had so mysteriously sunk into the ground : and here Sylvie drew a Magic Locket from its hiding-place, turned it over with a thoughtful air, and at last appealed to Bruno in a rather helpless way. "What *was* it we had to do with it, Bruno? It's all gone out of my head!"

"Kiss it!" was Bruno's invariable recipe in cases of doubt and difficulty. Sylvie kissed it, but no result followed.

"Rub it the wrong way," was Bruno's next suggestion.

"Which *is* the wrong way?" Sylvie most

reasonably enquired. The obvious plan was to try *both* ways.

Rubbing from left to right had no visible effect whatever.

From right to left—"Oh, stop, Sylvie!" Bruno cried in sudden alarm. "Whatever *is* going to happen?"

For a number of trees, on the neighbouring hillside, were moving slowly upwards, in solemn procession: while a mild little brook, that had been rippling at our feet a moment before, began to swell, and foam, and hiss, and bubble, in a truly alarming fashion.

"Rub it some other way!" cried Bruno. "Try up-and-down! Quick!"

It was a happy thought. Up-and-down did it: and the landscape, which had been showing signs of mental aberration in various directions, returned to its normal condition of sobriety—with the exception of a small yellowish-brown mouse, which continued to run wildly up and down the road, lashing its tail like a little lion.

"Let's follow it," said Sylvie: and this also turned out a happy thought. The mouse at once settled down into a business-like jog-trot, with which we could easily keep pace. The only phenomenon, that gave me any uneasiness, was the rapid increase in the *size* of the little creature we were following, which became every moment more and more like a real lion.

Soon the transformation was complete: and a noble lion stood patiently waiting for us to come up with it. No thought of fear seemed to occur to the children, who patted and stroked it as if it had been a Shetland-pony.

"Help me up!" cried Bruno. And in another moment Sylvie had lifted him upon the broad back of the gentle beast, and seated herself behind him, pillion-fashion. Bruno took a good handful of mane in each hand, and made believe to guide this new kind of steed. "Gee-up!" seemed quite sufficient by way of *verbal* direction: the lion at once broke into an easy canter, and we soon found ourselves in the depths of the forest. Sylvie and Bruno at the same moment dismounting.

Yes, we were in the garden once more: and to escape that horrid discordant voice, we hurried indoors, and found ourselves in the library—Uggug blubbering, the Professor stand-

Harry Furniss
SWAIN SC

ing by with a bewildered air, and my Lady, with her arms clasped round her son's neck, repeating, over and over again, "and *did* they give him nasty lessons to learn? My own pretty pet!"

"What's all this noise about?" the Vice-Warden angrily enquired, as he strode into the room. "And who put the hat-stand here?" And he hung his hat up on Bruno, who was standing in the middle of the room, too much astonished by the sudden change of scene to make any attempt at removing it, though it came down to his shoulders, making him look something like a small candle with a large extinguisher over it.

Having released himself from his extinguisher, Bruno rushed headlong out of the room, followed by Sylvie.

"We must go to Father!" Sylvie panted, as they ran down the garden. "I'm *sure* things are at their worst! I'll ask the Gardener to let us out again."

"But we ca'n't *walk* all the way!" Bruno whimpered. "How I *wiss* we had a coach-and-four, like Uncle!"

And, shrill and wild, rang through the air the familiar voice :—

> "*He thought he saw a Coach-and-Four*
> *That stood beside his bed:*
> *He looked again, and found it was*
> *A Bear without a Head.*
> *'Poor thing,' he said, 'poor silly thing!*
> *It's waiting to be fed!'*"

"No, I ca'n't let you out again!" he said, before the children could speak. "The Vice-Warden gave it me, he did, for letting you out last time! So be off with you!" And, turning away from them, he began digging frantically in the middle of a gravel-walk, singing, over and over again,

> "'*Poor thing,' he said, 'poor silly thing!*
> *It's waiting to be fed!*'"

but in a more musical tone than the shrill screech in which he had begun.

"We were looking for you!" cried Sylvie, to the Professor. "We *do* want you so much, you ca'n't think!"

"What is it, dear children?" the Professor asked, beaming on them with a very different look from what Uggug ever got from him.

"We want you to speak to the Gardener for us," Sylvie said, as she and Bruno took the old man's hands and led him into the hall.

"He's ever so unkind!" Bruno mournfully added. "They's *all* unkind to us, now that Father's gone. The Lion were *much* nicer!"

"But you must explain to me, please," the Professor said with an anxious look, "*which* is the Lion, and *which* is the Gardener. It's *most* important not to get two such animals confused together. And one's very liable to do it in their case—both having mouths, you know——"

"Doos oo *always* confuses two animals together?" Bruno asked.

"Pretty often, I'm afraid," the Professor candidly confessed. "Now, for instance, there's the rabbit-hutch and the hall-clock." The Professor pointed them out. "One gets a little confused with *them*—both having doors, you know. Now, only yesterday—would you believe it?—I put some lettuces into the clock, and tried to wind up the rabbit!"

"Did the rabbit *go*, after oo wounded it up?" said Bruno.

The Professor clasped his hands on the top of his head, and groaned. "Go? I should think it *did* go! Why, it's *gone!* And where ever its gone to—that's what I *can't* find out! I've done my best—I've read all the article 'Rabbit' in the great dictionary—Come in!"

"Only the tailor, Sir, with your little bill," said a meek voice outside the door.

"Ah, well, I can soon settle *his* business,"

the Professor said to the children, "if you'll just wait a minute. How much is it, this year, my man?" The tailor had come in while he was speaking.

"Well, it's been a doubling so many years, you see," the tailor replied, a little gruffly, "and I think I'd like the money now. It's two thousand pound, it is!"

"Oh, that's nothing!" the Professor carelessly remarked, feeling in his pocket, as if he always carried at least *that* amount about with him. "But wouldn't you like to wait just another year, and make it *four* thousand? Just think how rich you'd be! Why, you might be a *King*, if you liked!"

"I don't know as I'd care about being a *King*," the man said thoughtfully. "But it *dew* sound a powerful sight o' money! Well, I think I'll wait——"

"Of course you will!" said the Professor. "There's good sense in *you*, I see. Good-day to you, my man!"

"Will you ever have to pay him that four thousand pounds?" Sylvie asked as the door closed on the departing creditor.

"*Never*, my child!" the Professor replied emphatically. "He'll go on doubling it, till he dies. You see it's *always* worth while waiting another year, to get twice as much money!"

CHAPTER VI

THE OTHER PROFESSOR

"AND now what would you like to do, my little friends? Shall I take you to see the Other Professor? This would be an excellent opportunity for a visit," he said to himself, glancing at his watch: "he generally takes a short rest—of fourteen minutes and a half—about this time."

Bruno hastily went round to Sylvie, who was standing at the other side of the Professor, and put his hand into hers. "I *thinks* we'd like to go," he said doubtfully: "only please let's go all together. It's best to be on the safe side, oo know!"

"Why, you talk as if you were *Sylvie!*" exclaimed the Professor.

"I know I did," Bruno replied very humbly. "I quite forgotted I wasn't Sylvie. Only I fought he might be rarver fierce!"

The Professor laughed a jolly laugh. "Oh, he's quite tame!" he said. "He never bites. He's only a little—a little *dreamy*, you know." He took hold of Bruno's other hand, and led the children down a long passage I had never noticed before—not that there was anything remarkable in *that:* I was constantly coming on new rooms and passages in that mysterious Palace, and very seldom succeeded in finding the old ones again.

Near the end of the passage the Professor stopped. "This is his room," he said, pointing to the solid wall.

"We can't get in through *there!*" Bruno exclaimed.

Sylvie said nothing, till she had carefully examined whether the wall opened anywhere. Then she laughed merrily. "You're playing us a trick, you dear old thing!" she said. "There's no *door* here!"

"There isn't any door to the room," said the Professor. "We shall have to climb in at the window."

So we went into the garden, and soon found the window of the Other Professor's room. It was a ground-floor window, and stood invitingly open: the Professor first lifted the two children in, and then he and I climbed in after them.

The Other Professor was seated at a table, with a large book open before him, on which his forehead was resting: he had clasped his arms round the book, and was snoring heavily. "He usually reads like that," the Professor remarked, "when the book's very interesting: and then sometimes it's very difficult to get him to attend!"

This seemed to be one of the difficult times: the Professor lifted him up, once or twice, and shook him violently: but he always returned to his book the moment he was let go of, and showed by his heavy breathing that the book was as interesting as ever.

"How dreamy he is!" the Professor exclaimed. "He must have got to a *very*

interesting part of the book!" And he rained quite a shower of thumps on the Other Professor's back, shouting, "Hoy! Hoy!" all the time. "Isn't it *wonderful* that he should be so dreamy?" he said to Bruno.

"If he's always as *sleepy* as that," Bruno remarked, "a *course* he's dreamy!"

"But what are we to *do?*" said the Professor. "You see he's quite wrapped up in the book!"

"Suppose oo *shuts* the book?" Bruno suggested.

"That's it! cried the delighted Professor. "Of course that'll do it!" And he shut up the book so quickly that he caught the Other Professor's nose between the leaves, and gave it a severe pinch.

The other Professor instantly rose to his feet, and carried the book away to the end of the room, where he put it back in its place in the book-case. "I've been reading for eighteen hours and three-quarters," he said, "and now I shall rest for fourteen minutes and a half."

"And as to the 'Pig-Tale'—which *you* have so kindly promised to give us—" the

Professor said, thoughtfully rubbing his chin. "I think that had better come at the *end* of the Banquet: then people can listen to it quietly."

"Shall I *sing* it?" the Other Professor asked, with a smile of delight.

"If you *can*," the Professor replied cautiously.

"Let me try," said the Other Professor, seating himself at the pianoforte. "For the sake of argument, let us assume that it begins on A flat." And he struck the note in question. "La, la, la! I think that's within an octave of it." He struck the note again, and appealed to Bruno, who was standing at his side. "Did I sing it like *that*, my child?"

"No, oo didn't," Bruno replied with great decision. "It were more like a duck."

"Single notes are apt to have that effect," the Other Professor said with a sigh. "Let me try a whole verse.

There was a Pig, that sat alone,
Beside a ruined Pump.
By day and night he made his moan:
It would have stirred a heart of stone
To see him wring his hoofs and groan,
Because he could not jump.

Would you call that a tune, Professor?" he asked, when he had finished.

The Professor considered a little. "Well," he said at last, "some of the notes are the same as others—and some are different—but I should hardly call it a *tune*."

"Let me try it a bit by myself," said the Other Professor. And he began touching the notes here and there, and humming to himself like an angry bluebottle.

"How do you like his singing?" the Professor asked the children in a low voice.

"It isn't very *beautiful*," Sylvie said, hesitatingly.

"It's very extremely *ugly!*" Bruno said, without any hesitation at all.

"All extremes are bad," the Professor said, very gravely. "For instance, Sobriety is a very good thing, when practised *in moderation*: but even Sobriety, when carried to an *extreme*, has its disadvantages."

"What are its disadvantages?" was the question that rose in my mind—and, as usual, Bruno asked it for me. "What *are* its lizard bandages?"

"Well, this is *one* of them," said the Professor. "When a man's tipsy (that's one extreme, you know), he sees one thing as two. But, when he's *extremely* sober (that's the other extreme), he sees two things as one. It's equally inconvenient, whichever happens."

"What does 'illconvenient' mean?" Bruno whispered to Sylvie.

"The difference between 'convenient' and 'inconvenient' is best explained by an example," said the Other Professor, who had overheard the question. "If you'll just think over any poem that contains the two words—such as——"

The Professor put his hands over his ears, with a look of dismay. "If you once let him begin a *Poem*," he said to Sylvie, "he'll never leave off again! He never does!"

"Did he ever begin a Poem and not leave off again?" Sylvie enquired.

"Three times," said the Professor.

Bruno raised himself on tiptoe, till his lips were on a level with Sylvie's ear. "What became of the three Poems?" he whispered. "Is he saying them all, now?"

"Hush!" said Sylvie. "The Other Professor is speaking!"

"I'll say it very quick," murmured the Other Professor, with downcast eyes, and melancholy voice, which contrasted oddly with his face, as he had forgotten to leave off smiling. ("At least it wasn't exactly a *smile*," as Sylvie said afterwards: "it looked as if his mouth was made that shape.")

"Go on, then," said the Professor. "*What must be must be.*"

"Remember that;" Sylvie whispered to Bruno. "It's a very good rule for whenever you hurt yourself."

"And it's a very good rule for whenever I make a noise," said the saucy little fellow. "So *you* remember it too, Miss!"

"Whatever *do* you mean?" said Sylvie, trying to frown, a thing she never managed particularly well.

"Oftens and oftens," said Bruno, "haven't oo told me 'There mustn't be so much noise, Bruno!' when I've tolded oo 'There *must!*' Why, there isn't no rules at all about 'There mustn't!' But oo never believes *me!*"

"As if anyone *could* believe *you*, you wicked, wicked boy!" said Sylvie. The *words* were severe enough, but I am of opinion that, when you are really *anxious* to impress a criminal with a sense of his guilt, you ought not to pronounce the sentence with your lips *quite* close to his cheek—since a kiss at the end of it, however accidental, weakens the effect terribly.

But just then he seemed, I fancied, a little exhausted. In fact, he climbed up into Sylvie's lap as he spoke, and rested his head against her shoulder.

CHAPTER VII

RULES

The Other Professor regarded him with some anxiety. "The smaller animal ought to go to bed *at once*," he said with an air of authority.

"Why *at once?*" said the Professor.

"Because he can't go at twice," said the Other Professor.

The Professor gently clapped his hands. "Isn't he *wonderful!*" he said to Sylvie. "Nobody else could have thought of the reason so quick. Why, *of course* he ca'n't go at twice! It would hurt him to be divided."

This remark woke up Bruno, suddenly and completely. "I don't want to be *divided*," he said decisively.

"It does very well on a *diagram*," said the Other Professor. "I could show it you in a minute, only the chalk's a little blunt."

"Take care!" Sylvie anxiously exclaimed, as he began, rather clumsily, to point it. "You'll cut your finger off, if you hold the knife so!"

"If oo cuts it off, will oo give it to *me*, please?" Bruno thoughtfully added.

"It's like this," said the Other Professor, hastily drawing a long line upon the black board, and marking th letters '*A*,' '*B*,' at the two ends, and '*C*' in the middle: "let me explain it to you. If *AB* were to be divided into two parts at *C*——"

"It would be drownded," Bruno pronounced confidently.

The Other Professor gasped. "*What* would be drownded?"

"Why the bumble-bee, of course!" said Bruno. "And the two bits would sink down in the sea!"

Here the Professor interfered, as the Other Professor was evidently too much puzzled to go on with his diagram.

"When I said it would *hurt* him, I was merely referring to the action of the nerves——"

The Other Professor brightened up in a moment. "The action of the nerves," he began eagerly, "is curiously slow in some people. I had a friend once, that, if you burnt him with a red-hot poker, it would take years and years before he felt it!"

"And if you only *pinched* him?" queried Sylvie.

"Then it would take ever so much longer, of course. In fact, I doubt if the man *himself* would ever feel it, at all. His grandchildren might."

"I wouldn't like to be the grandchild of a pinched grandfather, would *you*, Mister Sir?" Bruno whispered. "It might come just when you wanted to be happy!"

That would be awkward, I admitted, taking it quite as a matter of course that he had so suddenly caught sight of me. "But don't you *always* want to be happy, Bruno?"

"Not *always*," Bruno said thoughtfully. "Sometimes when I's *too* happy, I wants to be a little miserable. Then I just tell Sylvie about it, oo know, and Sylvie sets me some lessons. Then it's all right."

"I'm sorry you don't like lessons," I said. "You should copy Sylvie. *She's* always as busy as the day is long!"

"Well, so am *I!*" said Bruno.

"No, no!" Sylvie corrected him. "*You're* as busy as the day is *short!*"

"Well, what's the difference?" Bruno asked. "Mister Sir, isn't the day as short as it's long? I mean, isn't it the *same* length?"

Never having considered the question in this light, I suggested that they had better ask the Professor; and they ran off in a moment to appeal to their old friend. The Professor left off polishing his spectacles to consider. "My dears," he said after a minute, "the day is the same length as anything that is the same length as *it*." And he resumed his never-ending task of polishing.

The children returned, slowly and thoughtfully, to report his answer. "*Isn't* he wise?" Sylvie asked in an awe-struck whisper. "If *I* was as wise as *that*, I should have a head-ache all day long. I *know* I should!"

"You appear to be talking to somebody—that isn't here," the Professor said, turning round to the children. "Who is it?"

Bruno looked puzzled. "I never talks to nobody when he isn't here!" he replied. "It isn't good manners. Oo should always wait till he comes, before oo talks to him!"

The Professor looked anxiously in my direction, and seemed to look through and through me without seeing me. "Then who are you talking to?" he said. "There isn't anybody here, you know, except the Other Professor—and *he* isn't here!" he added wildly, turning round and round like a teetotum. "Children! Help to look for him! Quick! He's got lost again!"

The children were on their feet in a moment.

"Where shall we look?" said Sylvie.

"Anywhere!" shouted the excited Professor. "Only be quick about it!" And he began trotting round and round the room, lifting up the chairs, and shaking them.

Bruno took a very small book out of the bookcase, opened it, and shook it in imitation of the Professor. "He isn't *here*," he said.

"He *ca'n't* be there, Bruno!" Sylvie said indignantly.

"Course he ca'n't!" said Bruno. "I should have shooked him out, if he'd been in there!"

"Has he ever been lost before?" Sylvie enquired, turning up a corner of the hearth-rug, and peeping under it.

"Once before," said the Professor: "he once lost himself in a wood——"

"And couldn't he find his-self again?" said Bruno. "Why didn't he shout? He'd be sure to hear his-self, 'cause he couldn't be far off, oo know."

"Let's try shouting," said the Professor.

"What shall we shout?" said Sylvie.

"On second thoughts, *don't* shout," the Professor replied. "The Vice-Warden might hear you. He's getting awfully strict!"

This reminded the poor children of all the troubles, about which they had come to their old friend. Bruno sat down on the floor and began crying. "He *is* so cruel!" he sobbed. "And he lets Uggug take away *all* my toys! And such horrid meals!"

"What did you have for dinner to-day?" said the Professor.

"A little piece of a dead crow," was Bruno's mournful reply.

"He means rook-pie," Sylvie explained.

"It *were* a dead crow," Bruno persisted. "And there were a apple-pudding—and Uggug ate it all—and I got nuffin but a crust! And I asked for a orange—and—didn't get it!" And the poor little fellow buried his face in Sylvie's lap, who kept gently stroking his hair, as she went on. "It's all true, Professor, dear! They *do* treat my darling Bruno very badly! And they're not kind to *me* either," she added in a lower tone, as if *that* were a thing of much less importance.

The Professor got out a large red silk handkerchief, and wiped his eyes. "I wish I could help you, dear children!" he said. "But what *can* I do?"

"We know the way to Fairyland—where Father's gone—quite well," said Sylvie: "if only the Gardener would let us out."

"Won't he open the door for you?" said the Professor.

"Not for *us*," said Sylvie: "but I'm sure he would for *you*. Do come and ask him, Professor, dear!"

"I'll come this minute!" said the Professor.

Bruno sat up and dried his eyes. "*Isn't* he kind, Mister Sir?"

"He is *indeed*," said I. But the Professor took no notice of my remark. He had put on a beautiful cap with a long tassel, and was selecting one of the Other Professor's walking-sticks, from a stand in the corner of the room. "A thick stick in one's hand makes people respectful," he was saying to himself. "Come along, dear children!" And we all went out into the garden together.

"I shall address him, first of all," the Professor exclaimed as we went along, "with a few playful remarks on the weather. I shall then question him about the Other Professor. This will have a double advantage. First, it will open the conversation (you can't even drink a bottle of wine without opening it first): and secondly, if he's seen the Other Professor, we shall find him that way: and, if he hasn't, we sha'n't."

We had no sort of difficulty in *finding* the Gardener. Though he was hidden from us by some trees, that harsh voice of his served to direct us; and, as we drew nearer, the words of his song became more and more plainly audible:—

> " *He thought he saw an Albatross*
> *That fluttered round the lamp:*
> *He looked again, and found it was*
> *A Penny-Postage-Stamp.*
> ' *You'd best be getting home,' he said:*
> ' *The nights are very damp!* ' "

"Would it be afraid of catching cold?" said Bruno.

"If it got *very* damp," Sylvie suggested, "it might stick to something, you know."

"And *that* somefin would have to go by the post, whatever it was!" Bruno eagerly exclaimed. "Suppose it was a cow! Wouldn't it be *dreadful* for the other things!"

"And all these things happened to *him*," said the Professor. "That's what makes the song so interesting."

"He must have had a very curious life," said Sylvie.

"You may say that!" the Professor heartily rejoined.

"Of course she may!" cried Bruno.

By this time we had come up to the Gardener, who was standing on one leg, as usual, and busily employed in watering a bed of flowers with an empty watering-can.

"It hasn't got no water in it!" Bruno explained to him, pulling his sleeve to attract his attention.

"It's lighter to hold," said the Gardener. "A lot of water in it makes one's arms ache." And he went on with his work, singing softly to himself.

"The nights are very damp!"

"In digging things out of the ground—

which you probably do now and then," the Professor began in a loud voice; "in making things into heaps—which no doubt you often do; and in kicking things about with one heel—which you seem never to leave off doing; have you ever happened to notice another Professor, something like me, but different?"

"Never!" shouted the Gardener, so loudly and violently that we all drew back in alarm. "There ain't such a thing!"

"We will try a less exciting topic," the Professor mildly remarked to the children. "You were asking——"

"We asked him to let us through the garden-door," said Sylvie: "but he wouldn't: but perhaps he would for *you!*"

The Professor put the request very humbly and courteously.

"I wouldn't mind letting *you* out," said the Gardener. "But I mustn't open the door for *children.* D'you think I'd disobey the *Rules?* Not for one-and-sixpence!"

The Professor cautiously produced a couple of shillings.

"That'll do it!" the Gardener shouted, as

he hurled the watering-can across the flower-bed, and produced a handful of keys—one large one, and a number of small ones.

"But look here, Professor, dear!" whispered Sylvie. "He needn't open the door for *us*, at all. We can go out with *you*."

"True, dear child!" the Professor thankfully replied, as he replaced the coins in his pocket. "That saves two shillings!" And he took the children's hands, that they might all go out together when the door was opened. This, however, did not seem a very likely event, though the Gardener patiently tried all the small keys, over and over again.

At last the Professor ventured on a gentle suggestion. "Why not try the *large* one? I have often observed that a door unlocks *much* more nicely with its *own* key."

The very first trial of the large key proved a success: the Gardener opened the door, and held out his hand for the money.

The Professor shook his head. "You are acting by *Rule*," he explained, "in opening the door for *me*. And now it's open, we are going out by *Rule*—the Rule of *Three*."

The Gardener looked puzzled, and let us go out; but, as he locked the door behind us, we heard him singing thoughtfully to himself

"He thought he saw a Garden-Door
That opened with a key:
He looked again, and found it was
A Double Rule of Three:
'And all its mystery,' he said,
'Is clear as day to me!'"

"I shall now return," said the Professor, when we had walked a few yards: "you see, it's impossible to read *here*, for all my books are in the house."

But the children still kept fast hold of his hands. "*Do* come with us!" Sylvie entreated with tears in her eyes.

"Well, well!" said the good-natured old man. "Perhaps I'll come after you, some day soon. But I *must* go back *now*. You see I left off at a comma, and it's so awkward not knowing how the sentence finishes! Besides, you've got to go through Dogland first, and I'm always a little nervous about dogs. But it'll be quite easy to come, as soon as I've completed my new invention—for carrying one's-*self*, you know. It wants just a *little* more working out."

"Won't that be very tiring, to carry *yourself?*" Sylvie enquired.

"Well, no, my child. You see, whatever fatigue one incurs by *carrying*, one saves by *being carried!* Good-bye, dears!"

CHAPTER VIII

DOGLAND

"THERE'S a house, away there to the left," said Sylvie, after we had walked what seemed to me about fifty miles. "Let's go and ask for a night's lodging."

"It looks a very comfable house," Bruno said, as we turned into the road leading up to it. "I doos hope the Dogs will be kind to us, I *is* so tired and hungry!"

A Mastiff, dressed in a scarlet collar, and carrying a musket, was pacing up and down, like a sentinel, in front of the entrance. He started, on catching sight of the children, and came forwards to meet them, keeping his musket pointed straight at Bruno, who stood quite still, though he turned pale and kept tight hold of Sylvie's hand, while the Sentinel walked solemnly round and round them, and looked at them from all points of view.

"Oobooh, hooh boohooyah!" He growled at last. "Woobah yahwah oobooh! Bow wahbah woobooyah? Bow wow?" he asked Bruno severely.

Of course *Bruno* understood all this, easily enough. All Fairies understand Doggee—that is, Dog-language. But, as *you* may find it a little difficult, just at first, I had better put it into English for you. "Humans, I verily believe! A couple of stray Humans! What Dog do you belong to? What do you want?"

"We don't belong to a *Dog!*" Bruno began, in Doggee. ("Peoples *never* belongs to Dogs!" he whispered to Sylvie.)

But Sylvie hastily checked him, for fear of hurting the Mastiff's feelings. "Please, we want a little food, and a night's lodging—if there's room in the house," she added timidly. Sylvie spoke Doggee very prettily: but I think it's almost better, for *you*, to give the conversation in English.

"The *house*, indeed!" growled the Sentinel. "Have you never seen a *Palace* in your life? Come along with me! His Majesty must settle what's to be done with you."

They followed him through the entrance-hall, down a long passage, and into a magnificent Saloon, around which were grouped dogs of all sorts and sizes. Two splendid Blood-hounds were solemnly sitting up, one on each side of the crown-bearer. Two or three Bull-dogs—whom I guessed to be the Body-Guard of the

King—were waiting in grim silence: in fact the only voices at all plainly audible were those of two little dogs, who had mounted a settee, and were holding a lively discussion that looked very like a quarrel.

"Lords and Ladies in Waiting, and various Court Officials," our guide gruffly remarked, as he led us in. Of *me* the Courtiers took no notice whatever: but Sylvie and Bruno were the subject of many inquisitive looks, and many whispered remarks, of which I only distinctly caught *one*—made by a sly-looking Dachshund to his friend—"Bah wooh wahyah hoobah Oobooh, *hah* bah?" ("She's not such a bad-looking Human, *is* she?")

Leaving the new arrivals in the centre of the Saloon, the Sentinel advanced to a door, at the further end of it, which bore an inscription, painted on it in Doggee, "Royal Kennel—Scratch and Yell."

Before doing this, the Sentinel turned to the children, and said "Give me your names."

"We'd rather not!" Bruno exclaimed, pulling Sylvie away from the door. "We want them ourselves. Come back, Sylvie! Come quick!"

"Nonsense!" said Sylvie very decidedly: and gave their names in Doggee.

Then the Sentinel scratched violently at the door, and gave a yell that made Bruno shiver from head to foot.

"Hooyah wah!" said a deep voice inside. (That's Doggee for "Come in!")

"It's the King himself!" the Mastiff whispered in an awestruck tone. "Take off your wigs, and lay them humbly at his paws." (What *we* should call "at his *feet*.")

Sylvie was just going to explain, very politely, that really they *couldn't* perform *that* ceremony, because their wigs wouldn't come off, when the door of the Royal Kennel opened, and an enormous Newfoundland Dog put his head out. "Bow wow?" was his first question.

"When His Majesty speaks to you," the Sentinel hastily whispered to Bruno, "you should prick up your ears!"

Bruno looked doubtfully at Sylvie. "I'd rather not, please," he said. "It would hurt."

"It doesn't hurt a bit!" the Sentinel said with some indignation. "Look! It's like this!"

And he pricked up his ears like two railway signals.

Sylvie gently explained matters. "I'm afraid we ca'n't manage it," she said in a low voice. "I'm very sorry: but our ears haven't got the right—" she wanted to say "machinery" in Doggee: but she had forgotten the word, and could only think of "steam-engine."

The Sentinel repeated Sylvie's explanation to the King.

"Ca'n't prick up their ears without a steam-engine!" His Majesty exclaimed. "They *must* be curious creatures! I must have a look at them!" And he came out of his Kennel, and walked solemnly up to the children.

What was the amazement—not to say the horror—of the whole assembly, when Sylvie actually *patted His Majesty on the head*, while Bruno seized his long ears and pretended to tie them together under his chin!

The Sentinel groaned aloud: a beautiful Greyhound—who appeared to be one of the Ladies in Waiting—fainted away: and all the other Courtiers hastily drew back, and left plenty of room for the huge Newfoundland to

SWAIN Sc
Harry Furniss

spring upon the audacious strangers, and tear them limb from limb.

Only—he didn't. On the contrary His Majesty actually *smiled*—so far as a dog *can* smile—and (the other Dogs couldn't believe their eyes, but it was true, all the same) his Majesty *wagged his tail!*

"Yah! Hooh hahwooh!" (that is "Well! I never!") was the universal cry.

His Majesty looked round him severely, and gave a slight growl, which produced instant silence. "Conduct *my friends* to the banqueting-hall!" he said, laying such an emphasis on "*my friends*" that several of the dogs rolled over helplessly on their backs and began to lick Bruno's feet.

A procession was formed, but I only ventured to follow as far as the *door* of the banqueting-hall, so furious was the uproar of barking dogs within. So I sat down by the King, who seemed to have gone to sleep, and waited till the children returned to say good-night, when His Majesty got up and shook himself.

"Time for bed!" he said with a sleepy yawn. "The attendants will show you your room," he added, aside, to Sylvie and Bruno. "Bring lights!" And, with a dignified air, he held out his paw for them to kiss.

But the children were evidently not well practised in Court-manners. Sylvie simply stroked the great paw: Bruno hugged it: the Master of the Ceremonies looked shocked.

The next thing I remember is that it was morning: breakfast was just over: Sylvie was lifting Bruno down from a high chair, and saying to a Spaniel, who was regarding them with a most benevolent smile, "Yes, thank you, we've had a *very* nice breakfast. Haven't we, Bruno?"

"There was too many bones in the——" Bruno began, but Sylvie frowned at him, and laid her finger on her lips, for, at this moment, the travellers were waited on by a very dignified officer, the Head-Growler, whose duty it was, first to conduct them to the King to bid him farewell, and then to escort them to the boundary of Dogland. The great Newfoundland received them most affably, but, instead of saying "good-bye," he startled the Head-Growler into giving three savage growls, by announcing that he would escort them himself.

"It is a most unusual proceeding, your Majesty!" the Head-Growler exclaimed, almost choking with vexation at being set aside, for he had put on his best Court-suit, made entirely of cat-skins, for the occasion.

"I shall escort them myself," His Majesty repeated, gently but firmly, laying aside the Royal robes, and changing his crown for a small coronet, "and you may stay at home."

"I *are* glad!" Bruno whispered to Sylvie, when they had got well out of hearing. "He were so *welly* cross!" And he not only patted their Royal escort, but even hugged him round the neck in the exuberance of his delight.

His Majesty calmly wagged the Royal tail. "It's quite a relief," he said, "getting away from that Palace now and then! Royal Dogs have a dull life of it, I can tell you! Would you mind" (this to Sylvie, in a low voice, and looking a little shy and embarrassed), "would you mind the trouble of just throwing that stick for me to fetch?"

Sylvie was too much astonished to do anything for a moment: it sounded such a monstrous impossibility that a *King* should wish to run after a stick. But *Bruno* was equal to the occasion, and with a glad shout of "Hi then! Fetch it, good Doggie!" he hurled it over a clump of bushes. The next moment the Monarch of Dogland had bounded over the bushes, and picked up the stick, and came galloping back to the children with it in his mouth. Bruno took it from him with great decision. "Beg for it!" he insisted; and His Majesty begged. "Paw!" commanded Sylvie! and His Majesty gave his paw. In short, the solemn ceremony of escorting the travellers to the boundaries of Dogland became one long uproarious game of play!

"But business is business!" the Dog-King said at last. "And I must go back to mine. I couldn't come any further," he added, consulting a dog-watch, which hung on a chain round his neck, "not even if there were a *Cat* in sight!"

They took an affectionate farewell of His Majesty, and trudged on.

"That *were* a dear dog!" Bruno exclaimed. "Has we to go far, Sylvie? I's tired!"

"Not much further, darling!" Sylvie gently

replied. "Do you see that shining, just beyond those trees? I'm almost *sure* it's the gate of Fairyland! I know it's all golden—Father told me so—and so bright, so bright!" she went on dreamily.

I could but stand outside, and take a last look at the two sweet children, ere they disappeared within, and the golden gate closed with a bang.

CHAPTER IX

FAIRIES

THE first thing I noticed, as I went lazily along through an open place in the wood, was a large Beetle lying struggling on its back, and I went down upon one knee to help the poor thing to its feet again, and was just reaching out a little stick to turn the Beetle over, when I saw a sight that made me draw back hastily and hold my breath, for fear of making any noise and frightening the little creature away.

Not that she looked as if she would be easily frightened; she seemed so good and gentle that I'm sure she would never expect that any one could wish to hurt her. She was only a few inches high, and was dressed in green, so that you really would hardly have noticed her among the long grass; and she was so delicate and graceful that she quite seemed to belong to the place, almost as if she were one of the flowers. I may tell you,

besides, that she had no wings (I don't believe in Fairies with wings), and that she had quantities of long brown hair and large earnest brown eyes, and then I shall have done all I can to give you an idea of her.

Sylvie (I found out her name afterwards) had knelt down, just as I was doing, to help the Beetle; but it needed more than a little stick for *her* to get it on its legs again; it was as much as she could do, with both arms, to roll the heavy thing over; and all the while she was talking to it, half scolding and half comforting, as a nurse might do with a child that had fallen down.

"There, there! You needn't cry so much about it. You're not killed yet—though if you were, you couldn't cry, you know, and so it's a general rule against crying, my dear! And how did you come to tumble over? But I can see well enough how it was—I needn't ask you that—walking over sand-pits with your chin in the air, as usual. Of course if you go among sand-pits like that, you must expect to tumble. You should look."

The Beetle murmured something that sounded like "I *did* look," and Sylvie went on again.

"But I know you didn't! You never do! You always walk with your chin up—you're so dreadfully conceited. Well, let's see how many legs are broken this time. Why, none of them, I declare! And what's the good of having six legs, my dear, if you can only kick them all about in the air when you tumble? Legs are meant to walk with, you know. Now don't begin putting out your wings yet; I've more to say. Go to the frog that lives behind that buttercup—give him my compliments—Sylvie's compliments—can you say 'compliments'?"

The Beetle tried and, I suppose, succeeded.

"Yes, that's right. And tell him he's to give you some of that salve I left with him yesterday. And you'd better get him to rub it in for you. He's got rather cold hands, but you mustn't mind that."

I think the Beetle must have shuddered at this idea, for Sylvie went on in a graver tone. "Now you needn't pretend to be so particular as all that, as if you were too grand to be rubbed by a frog. The fact is, you ought to be very much obliged to him. Suppose you could get nobody but a toad to do it, how would you like *that?*"

There was a little pause, and then Sylvie added, "Now you may go. Be a good beetle, and don't keep your chin in the air." And then began one of those performances of humming, and whizzing, and restless banging about, such as a beetle indulges in when it has decided on flying, but hasn't quite made up its mind which way to go. At last, in one of its awkward zig-zags, it managed to fly right into my face, and, by the time I had recovered from the shock, the little Fairy was gone.

I walked on sadly enough, you may be sure. However, I comforted myself with thinking "It's been a very wonderful afternoon, so far. I'll just go quietly on and look about me, and I shouldn't wonder if I were to come across another Fairy somewhere."

By this time the 'eerie' feeling had come back again; so I felt quite sure that "Bruno" was somewhere very near.

And so indeed he was—so near that I had very nearly walked over him without seeing him; which would have been dreadful, always supposing that Fairies *can* be walked over—my own belief is that they are something of the nature of Will-o'-the-Wisps: and there's no walking over *them*.

Think of any pretty little boy you know, with rosy cheeks, large dark eyes, and tangled brown hair, and then fancy him made small enough to go comfortably into a coffee-cup, and you'll have a very fair idea of him.

"What's your name, little one?" I began, in as soft a voice as I could manage.

"What's oors?" he said, without looking up.

I told him my name quite gently, for he was much too small to be angry with.

"Duke of Anything?" he asked, just looking at me for a moment, and then going on with his work.

"Not Duke at all," I said, a little ashamed of having to confess it.

"Oo're big enough to be two Dukes," said the little creature. "I suppose oo're Sir Something, then?"

"No," I said, feeling more and more ashamed. "I haven't got any title."

The Fairy seemed to think that in that case I really wasn't worth the trouble of talking to, for he quietly went on digging, and tearing the flowers to pieces.

After a few minutes I tried again. "*Please* tell me what your name is."

"Bruno," the little fellow answered, very readily. "Why didn't oo say 'please' before?"

"That's something like what we used to be taught in the nursery," I thought to myself, And here an idea came into my head, and I asked him "Aren't you one of the Fairies that teach children to be good?"

"Well, we have to do that sometimes," said Bruno, "and a dreadful bother it is." As he said this, he savagely tore a heartsease in two, and trampled on the pieces.

CHAPTER X

BRUNO'S REVENGE

"WHAT *are* you doing there, Bruno?" I said.

"Spoiling Sylvie's garden," was all the answer Bruno would give at first. But, as he went on tearing up the flowers, he muttered to himself "The nasty cross thing—wouldn't let me go and play this morning,—said I must finish my lessons first—lessons, indeed! I'll vex her finely, though!"

"Oh, Bruno, you shouldn't do that!" I cried. "Don't you know that's revenge? And revenge is a wicked, cruel, dangerous thing!"

"River-edge?" said Bruno. "What a funny

word! I suppose oo call it cruel and dangerous 'cause, if oo wented too far and tumbleded in, oo'd get drownded."

"No, not river-edge," I explained: "re-venge" (saying the word very slowly).

"Oh!" said Bruno, opening his eyes very wide, but without trying to repeat the word.

"Come! Try and pronounce it, Bruno!" I said, cheerfully. "Re-venge, re-venge."

But Bruno only tossed his little head, and said he couldn't; that his mouth wasn't the right shape for words of that kind. And the more I laughed, the more sulky the little fellow got about it.

"Well, never mind, my little man!" I said. "Shall I help you with that job?"

"Yes, please," Bruno said, quite pacified. "Only I wiss I could think of somefin to vex her more than this. Oo don't know how hard it is to make her angry!"

"Now listen to me, Bruno, and I'll teach you quite a splendid kind of revenge!"

"Somefin that'll vex her finely?" he asked with gleaming eyes.

"Something that will vex her finely. First,

we'll get up all the weeds in her garden. See, there are a good many at this end—quite hiding the flowers."

"But *that* won't vex her!" said Bruno.

"After that," I said, without noticing the remark, "we'll water this highest bed—up here. You see it's getting quite dry and dusty."

Bruno looked at me inquisitively, but he said nothing this time.

"Then after that," I went on, "the walks want sweeping a bit; and I think you might cut down that tall nettle—it's so close to the garden that it's quite in the way——"

"What *is* oo talking about?" Bruno impatiently interrupted me. "All that won't vex her a bit!"

"Won't it?" I said, innocently. "Then, after that, suppose we put in some of these coloured pebbles—just to mark the divisions between the different kinds of flowers, you know. That'll have a very pretty effect."

Bruno turned round and had another good stare at me. At last there came an odd little twinkle into his eyes, and he said, with quite a new meaning in his voice, "That'll do nicely. Let's put 'em in rows—all the red together, and all the blue together."

"That'll do capitally," I said; "and then—what kind of flowers does Sylvie like best?"

Bruno had to put his thumb in his mouth and consider a little before he could answer. "Violets," he said, at last.

"There's a beautiful bed of violets down by the brook——"

"Oh, let's fetch em!" cried Bruno, giving a little skip into the air. "Here! Catch hold of my hand, and I'll help oo along. The grass is rather thick down that way."

"No, not yet, Bruno," I said: "we must consider what's the right thing to do first. You see we've got quite a business before us."

"Yes, let's consider," said Bruno, putting his thumb into his mouth again, and sitting down upon a dead mouse.

"What do you keep that mouse for?" I said. "You should either bury it, or else throw it into the brook."

"Why, it's to measure with!" cried Bruno.

"How ever would oo do a garden without one? We make each bed three mouses and a half long, and two mouses wide."

I stopped him, as he was dragging it off by the tail to show me how it was used, for I was half afraid the 'eerie' feeling might go off before we had finished the garden, and in that case I should see no more of him or Sylvie. "I think the best way will be for *you* to weed the beds, while *I* sort out these pebbles, ready to mark the walks with."

"That's it!" cried Bruno. "And I'll tell oo about the caterpillars while we work."

"Ah, let's hear about the caterpillars," I said, as I drew the pebbles together into a heap and began dividing them into colours.

And Bruno went on in a low, rapid tone, more as if he were talking to himself. "Yesterday I saw two little caterpillars, when I was sitting by the brook, just where oo go into the wood. They were quite green, and they had yellow eyes, and they didn't see *me*. And one of them had got a moth's wing to carry—a great brown moth's wing, oo know, all dry, with feathers. So he couldn't want it to eat,

I should think—perhaps he meant to make a cloak for the winter?"

"Perhaps," I said, for Bruno had twisted up the last word into a sort of question, and was looking at me for an answer.

One word was quite enough for the little fellow, and he went on merrily. "Well, and so he didn't want the other caterpillar to see the moth's wing, oo know—so what must he do but try to carry it with all his left legs, and he tried to walk on the other set. Of course he toppled over after that."

"After what?" I said, catching at the last word, for, to tell the truth, I hadn't been attending much.

"He toppled over," Bruno repeated, very gravely, "and if *oo* ever saw a caterpillar topple over, oo'd know it's a welly serious thing, and not sit grinning like that—and I sha'n't tell oo no more!"

"Indeed and indeed, Bruno, I didn't mean to grin. See, I'm quite grave again now."

But Bruno only folded his arms, and said "Don't tell *me.* I see a little twinkle in one of oor eyes—just like the moon."

"Why do you think I'm like the moon, Bruno?" I asked.

"Oor face is large and round like the moon," Bruno answered, looking at me thoughtfully. "It doosn't shine quite so bright—but it's more cleaner."

I couldn't help smiling at this. "You know I sometimes wash *my* face, Bruno. The moon never does that."

"Oh, doosn't she though!" cried Bruno; and he leant forwards and added in a solemn whisper, "The moon's face gets dirtier and dirtier every night, till it's black all across. And then, when it's dirty all over—*so*—" (he passed his hand across his own rosy cheeks as he spoke) "then she washes it."

"Then it's all clean again, isn't it?"

"Not all in a moment," said Bruno. "What a deal of teaching oo wants! She washes it little by little—only she begins at the other edge, oo know."

By this time he was sitting quietly on the dead mouse with his arms folded, and the weeding wasn't getting on a bit: so I had to say "Work first, pleasure afterwards: no more talking till that bed's finished."

After that we had a few minutes of silence, while I sorted out the pebbles, and amused myself with watching Bruno's plan of gardening. It was quite a new plan to me: he always measured each bed before he weeded it, as if he was afraid the weeding would make it shrink; and once, when it came out longer than he wished, he set to work to thump the mouse with his little fist, crying out "There now! It's all gone wrong again! Why don't oo keep oor tail straight when I tell oo!"

"I'll tell you what I'll do," Bruno said in a half-whisper, as we worked. "Oo like Fairies, don't oo?"

"Yes," I said: "of course I do, or I shouldn't have come here. I should have gone to some place where there are no Fairies."

Bruno laughed contemptuously. "Why, oo might as well say oo'd go to some place where there wasn't any air — supposing oo didn't like air!"

This was a rather difficult idea to grasp. I tried a change of subject. "You're nearly the first Fairy I ever saw. Have *you* ever seen any people besides me?"

"Plenty!" said Bruno. "We see 'em when we walk in the road."

"But they ca'n't see *you.* How is it they never tread on you?"

"Ca'n't *tread* on us," said Bruno, looking amused at my ignorance. "Why, suppose oo're walking, here— so —" (making little marks on the ground) "and suppose there's a Fairy—that's me—walking *here.* Very well then, oo put one foot here, and one foot here, so oo doosn't tread on the Fairy."

This was all very well as an explanation, but it didn't convince me. "Why shouldn't I put one foot *on* the Fairy?" I asked.

"I don't know *why,*" the little fellow said in a thoughtful tone. "But I know oo *wouldn't.* Nobody never walked on the top of a Fairy. Now I'll tell oo what I'll do, as oo're so fond of Fairies. I'll get oo an invitation to the Fairy-King's dinner-party. I know one of the head-waiters."

I couldn't help laughing at this idea. "Do the waiters invite the guests?" I asked.

"Oh, not *to sit down!*" Bruno said. "But to wait at table. Oo'd like that, wouldn't oo? To hand about plates, and so on."

"Well, but that's not so nice as sitting at the table, is it?"

"Of course it isn't," Bruno said, in a tone as if he rather pitied my ignorance; "but if oo're not even Sir Anything, oo ca'n't expect to be allowed to sit at the table, oo know."

I said, as meekly as I could, that I didn't expect it, but it was the only way of going to a dinner-party that I really enjoyed. And Bruno tossed his head, and said, in a rather offended tone, that I might do as I pleased—there were many he knew that would give their ears to go.

"Have you ever been yourself, Bruno?"

"They invited me once, last week," Bruno said, very gravely. "It was to wash up the soup-plates—no, the cheese-plates I mean—that was grand enough. And I waited at table. And I didn't hardly make only *one* mistake."

"What was it?" I said. "You needn't mind telling *me*."

"Only bringing scissors to cut the beef with," Bruno said carelessly. "But the grandest thing of all was, *I* fetched the King a glass of cider!"

"That *was* grand!" I said, biting my lip to keep myself from laughing.

"Wasn't it?" said Bruno, very earnestly. "Oo know it isn't every one that's had such an honour as *that!*"

"Oh, come here quick!" he cried, in a state of the wildest excitement. "Catch hold of his other horn! I ca'n't hold him more than a minute!"

He was struggling desperately with a great snail, clinging to one of its horns, and nearly breaking his poor little back in his efforts to drag it over a blade of grass.

I saw we should have no more gardening if I let this sort of thing go on, so I quietly took the snail away, and put it on a bank where he couldn't reach it. "We'll hunt it afterwards, Bruno," I said, "if you really want to catch it. I'll go snail-hunting myself some day."

"I should think oo wouldn't be so silly," said Bruno, "as to go snail-hunting by oorself. Why, oo'd never get the snail along, if oo hadn't somebody to hold on to his other horn!'

"Of course I sha'n't go *alone*," I said, quite gravely. "By the way, is that the best kind to hunt, or do you recommend the ones without shells?"

"Oh, no, we never hunt the ones without shells," Bruno said, with a little shudder at the thought of it. "They're always so cross about it; and then, if oo tumbles over them, they're ever so sticky!"

By this time we had nearly finished the garden. I had fetched some violets, and Bruno was just helping me to put in the last, when he suddenly stopped and said "I'm tired."

"Rest then," I said: "I can go on without you, quite well."

Bruno needed no second invitation: he at once began arranging the dead mouse as a kind of sofa. "And I'll sing oo a little song," he said, as he rolled it about.

"Do," said I: "I like songs very much."

"Which song will oo choose?" Bruno said, as he dragged the mouse into a place where he could get a good view of me. "'Ting, ting, ting,' is the nicest."

There was no resisting such a strong hint as

this: however, I pretended to think about it for a moment, and then said "Well, I like 'Ting ting, ting,' best of all."

"That shows oo're a good judge of music," Bruno said, with a pleased look. "How many

hare-bells would oo like?" And he put his thumb into his mouth to help me to consider.

As there was only one cluster of hare-bells within easy reach, I said very gravely that I thought one would do *this* time, and I picked it and gave it to him. Bruno ran his hand once or twice up and down the flowers, like a musician trying an instrument, producing a most delicious delicate tinkling as he did so.

When he had satisfied himself that the flowers were in tune, he seated himself on the dead mouse (he never seemed really comfortable anywhere else), and, looking up at me with a merry twinkle in his eyes, he began. By the way, the tune was rather a curious one, and you might like to try it for yourself, so here are the notes.

"*Rise, oh, rise! The daylight dies:*
The owls are hooting, ting, ting, ting!
Wake, oh, wake! Beside the lake
The elves are fluting, ting, ting, ting!
Welcoming our Fairy King,
We sing, sing, sing."

He sang the first four lines briskly and

merrily, making the hare-bells chime in time with the music; but the last two he sang quite slowly and gently, and merely waved the flowers backwards and forwards. Then he left off to explain. "The Fairy-King is Oberon, and he lives across the lake—and sometimes he comes in a little boat—and we go and meet him—and then we sing this song, you know."

"And then you go and dine with him?" I said, mischievously.

"Oo shouldn't talk," Bruno hastily said: "it interrupts the song so."

I said I wouldn't do it again.

"I never talk myself when I'm singing," he went on very gravely: "so *oo* shouldn't either." Then he tuned the hare-bells once more, and sang:—

"Hear, oh, hear! From far and near
The music stealing, ting, ting, ting!
Fairy bells adown the dells
Are merrily pealing, ting, ting, ting!
Welcoming our Fairy King,
We ring, ring, ring.

"See, oh, see! On every tree
What lamps are shining, ting, ting, ting!
They are eyes of fiery flies
To light our dining, ting, ting, ting!
Welcoming our Fairy King,
They swing, swing, swing.

"Haste, oh, haste, to take and taste
The dainties waiting, ting, ting, ting!
Honey-dew is stored——"

"Hush, Bruno!" I interrupted in a warning whisper. "She's coming!"

Bruno checked his song, and, as she slowly made her way through the long grass, he suddenly rushed out headlong at her like a little bull, shouting "Look the other way! Look the other way!"

"Which way?" Sylvie asked, in rather a frightened tone, as she looked round in all directions to see where the danger could be.

"*That* way!" said Bruno, carefully turning her round with her face to the wood. "Now, walk backwards — walk gently — don't be frightened: oo sha'n't trip!"

But Sylvie *did* trip notwithstanding: in fact

he led her, in his hurry, across so many little sticks and stones, that it was really a wonder the poor child could keep on her feet at all. But he was far too much excited to think of what he was doing.

I silently pointed out to Bruno the best place to lead her to, so as to get a view of the whole garden at once: it was a little rising ground, about the height of a potato; and, when they had mounted it, I drew back into the shade, that Sylvie mightn't see me.

I heard Bruno cry out triumphantly "*Now* oo may look!" and then followed a clapping of hands, but it was all done by Bruno himself. Sylvie was silent—she only stood and gazed with her hands clasped together, and I was half afraid she didn't like it after all.

Bruno too was watching her anxiously, and when she jumped down off the mound, and began wandering up and down the little walks, he cautiously followed her about, evidently anxious that she should form her own opinion of it all, without any hint from him. And when at last she drew a long breath, and gave her verdict—in a hurried whisper, and without the slightest regard to grammar—"It's the loveliest thing as I never saw in all my life before!" the little fellow looked as well pleased as if it had been given by all the judges and juries in England put together.

"And did you really do it all by yourself, Bruno?" said Sylvie. "And all for me?"

"I was helped a bit," Bruno began with a merry little laugh at her surprise. "We've been at it all the afternoon—I thought oo'd like——" and here the poor little fellow's lip began to quiver, and all in a moment he burst out crying, and running up to Sylvie he flung his arms passionately round her neck, and hid his face on her shoulder.

There was a little quiver in Sylvie's voice too as she whispered, "Why, what's the matter, darling?" and tried to lift up his head and kiss him.

But Bruno only clung to her, sobbing, and wouldn't be comforted till he had confessed. "I tried—to spoil oor garden—first—but I'll never—never——" and then came another burst of tears, which drowned the rest of the sentence. At last he got out the words "I liked—putting in the flowers—for *oo*, Sylvie —and I never was so happy before." And the rosy little face came up at last to be kissed, all wet with tears as it was.

Sylvie was crying too by this time, and she said nothing but "Bruno, dear!" and "*I* never was so happy before," though why these two children who had never been so happy before should both be crying was a mystery to *me*.

After that they went through the whole garden again, flower by flower, as if it were a long sentence they were spelling out, with kisses for commas, and a great hug by way of a full-stop when they got to the end.

"Doos oo know, that was my river-edge, Sylvie?" Bruno solemnly began.

Sylvie laughed merrily. "What *do* you mean?" she said. And she pushed back her heavy brown hair with both hands and looked at him with dancing eyes in which the big teardrops were still glittering.

Bruno drew in a long breath, and made up his mouth for a great effort. "I mean re—venge," he said: "now oo under'tand." And he looked so happy and proud at having said the word right at last, that I quite envied him. I rather think Sylvie didn't "under'tand" at all; but she gave him a little kiss on each cheek which seemed to do just as well.

The very last thing I saw of them was this —Sylvie was stooping down with her arms round Bruno's neck, and saying coaxingly in his ear, "Do you know, Bruno, I've quite forgotten that hard word. Do say it once more. Come! Only this once, dear!"

But Bruno wouldn't try it again.

CHAPTER XI

BRUNO'S SONGS

THE path through the wood had been made familiar to me, by many a solitary stroll, in my former visit to Elveston. "And this open place," I said to myself, "seems to have some memory about it I cannot distinctly recall—surely it is the very spot where I saw those Fairy-Children! But I hope there are no snakes about!" I mused aloud, taking my seat on a fallen tree. "I certainly do *not* like snakes—and I don't suppose *Bruno* likes them, either!"

"No, he *doesn't* like them!" said a demure little voice at my side. "He's not *afraid* of them, you know. But he doesn't *like* them. He says they're too waggly!"

Words fail me to describe the beauty of the little group—couched on a patch of moss, on the trunk of the fallen tree, that met my eager gaze : Sylvie reclining with her elbow buried in the moss, and her rosy cheek resting in the

palm of her hand, and Bruno stretched at her feet with his head in her lap.

"Too waggly ?" was all I could say in so sudden an emergency.

"I'm not praticular," Bruno said, carelessly : "but I *do* like straight animals best——"

"But you like a dog when it wags its tail,"

Sylvie interrupted. "You *know* you do, Bruno!"

"But there's more of a dog, isn't there, Mister Sir?" Bruno appealed to me. "*You* wouldn't like to have a dog if it hadn't got nuffin but a head and a tail?"

I admitted that a dog of that kind would be uninteresting.

"There *isn't* such a dog as that," Sylvie thoughtfully remarked.

"But there *would* be," cried Bruno, "if the Professor shortened it up for us!"

"Shortened it up?" I said. "That's something new. How does he do it?"

"He's got a curious machine——" Sylvie was beginning to explain.

"A *welly* curious machine," Bruno broke in, not at all willing to have the story thus taken out of his mouth, "and if oo puts in—somefinoruvver—at *one* end, oo know—and he turns the handle—and it comes out at the uvver end, oh, ever so short!"

"As short as short!" Sylvie echoed.

"And one day—when we was in Outland, oo know—before we came to Fairyland—

me and Sylvie took him a big Crocodile. And he shortened it up for us. And it *did* look so funny! And it kept looking round, and saying 'wherever *is* the rest of me got to?' And then its eyes looked unhappy——"

"Not *both* its eyes," Sylvie interrupted.

"Course not!" said the little fellow. "Only the eye that *couldn't* see wherever the rest of it had got to. But the eye that *could* see wherever——"

"How short *was* the crocodile?" I asked, as the story was getting a little complicated.

"Half as short again as when we caught it —*so* long," said Bruno, spreading out his arms to their full stretch.

"But you didn't leave the poor thing so short as that, did you?"

"Well, no. Sylvie and me took it back again and we got it stretched to—to—how much was it, Sylvie?"

"Two times and a half, and a little bit more," said Sylvie.

"It wouldn't like that better than the other way, I'm afraid?"

"Oh, but it did though!" Bruno put in

eagerly. "It *were* proud of its new tail! Oo never saw a Crocodile so proud! Why, it could go round and walk on the top of its tail, and along its back, all the way to its head!"

"Not *quite* all the way," said Sylvie. "It couldn't, you know."

"Ah, but it *did*, once!" Bruno cried triumphantly. "Oo weren't looking—but *I* watched it. And it walked on tipplety-toe, so as it wouldn't wake itself, 'cause it thought it were asleep. And it got both its paws on its tail. And it walked and it walked all the way along its back. And it walked and it walked on its forehead. And it walked a tiny little way down its nose! There now!"

"I don't believe no Crocodile never walked along its own forehead!" Sylvie cried, too much excited by the controversy to limit the number of her negatives.

"Oo don't know the *reason* why it did it!" Bruno scornfully retorted. "It had a welly good reason. I *heerd* it say 'Why *shouldn't* I walk on my own forehead?' So a course it *did*, oo know!"

"If *that's* a good reason, Bruno," I said, "why shouldn't *you* get up that tree?"

"*Shall*, in a minute," said Bruno: "soon as we've done talking. Only two peoples *ca'n't* talk comfably togevver, when one's getting up a tree, and the other isn't!"

It appeared to me that a conversation would scarcely be 'comfable' while trees were being climbed, even if *both* the 'peoples' were doing it: but it was evidently dangerous to oppose any theory of Bruno's; so I thought it best to let the question drop, and to ask for an account of the machine that made things *longer*.

This time Bruno was at a loss, and left it to Sylvie. "It's like a mangle," she said: "if things are put in, they get squoze——"

"Squeezeled!" Bruno interrupted.

"Yes." Sylvie accepted the correction, but

did not attempt to pronounce the word, which was evidently new to her. "They get—like that—and they come out, oh, ever so long!"

"Once," Bruno began again, "Sylvie and me writed——"

"Wrote!" Sylvie whispered.

"Well, we *wroted* a Nursery-Song, and the Professor mangled it longer for us. It were '*There was a little Man, And he had a little gun, And the bullets*——'"

"I know the rest," I interrupted. "But would you say it *long*—I mean the way that it came *out* of the mangle?"

"We'll get the Professor to *sing* it for you," said Sylvie. "It would spoil it to *say* it."

"I would like to meet the Professor," I said. "And I would like to take you all with me, to see some friends of mine, that live near here. Would you like to come?"

"I don't think the *Professor* would like to come," said Sylvie. "He's *very* shy. But *we'd* like it very much. Only we'd better not come *this* size, you know."

The difficulty had occurred to me already: and I had felt that perhaps there *would* be a slight awkwardness in introducing two such tiny friends into Society. "What size will you be?" I enquired.

"We'd better come as—common *children*," Sylvie thoughtfully replied. "That's the easiest size to manage."

"Could you come to-day?" I said, thinking "then we could have you at the picnic!"

Sylvie considered a little. "Not *to-day*," she replied. "We haven't got the things ready. We'll come on—Tuesday next, if you like. And now, *really*, Bruno, you must come and do your lessons."

"I *wiss* oo wouldn't say '*really* Bruno!'" the little fellow pleaded, with pouting lips that made him look prettier than ever. "It *always* shows there's something horrid coming! And I won't kiss you, if you're so unkind."

"Ah, but you *have* kissed me!" Sylvie exclaimed in merry triumph.

"Well then, I'll *un*kiss you!" And he threw his arms around her neck for this novel, but apparently not *very* painful, operation.

"It's *very* like *kissing!*" Sylvie remarked, as soon as her lips were again free for speech.

"Oo don't know *nuffin* about it! It were just the *conkery!*" Bruno replied with much severity, as he marched away, and began at once

"There be three Badgers on a mossy stone
Beside a dark and covered way:
Each dreams himself a monarch on his throne,
And so they stay and stay—
Though their old Father languishes alone,
They stay, and stay, and stay.

"There be three Herrings loitering around,
Longing to share that mossy seat:

Each Herring tries to sing what she has found
That makes Life seem so sweet.
Thus, with a grating and uncertain sound,
They bleat, and bleat, and bleat.

"*The Mother-Herring, on the salt sea-wave,*
Sought vainly for her absent ones:
The Father-Badger, writhing in a cave,
Shrieked out 'Return, my sons!
You shall have buns,' he shrieked, 'if you'll behave!
Yea, buns, and buns, and buns!'

"'*I fear,' said she, 'your sons have gone astray?*
My daughters left me while I slept.'
'Yes 'm,' the Badger said: 'it's as you say.
'They should be better kept.'
Thus the poor parents talked the time away,
And wept, and wept, and wept."

Here Bruno broke off suddenly. "The Herrings' Song wants anuvver tune, Sylvie," he said. "And I ca'n't sing it—not wizout oo plays it for me!"

Instantly Sylvie seated herself upon a tiny mushroom, that happened to grow in front of a daisy, as if it were the most ordinary musical instrument in the world, and played on the petals as if they were the notes of an organ. And such delicious *tiny* music it was! Such teeny-tiny music!

Bruno held his head on one side, and listened

very gravely for a few moments until he had caught the melody. Then the sweet childish voice rang out once more:---

"*Oh, dear beyond our dearest dreams*
Fairer than all that fairest seems!

To feast the rosy hours away,
To revel in a roundelay!
How blest would be
A life so free—
Ipwergis-Pudding to consume,
And drink the subtle Azzigoom!

"*And if, in other days and hours,*
Mid other fluffs and other flowers,
The choice were given me how to dine—
'*Name what thou wilt: it shall be thine!*
Oh, then I see
The life for me—
Ipwergis-Pudding to consume,
And drink the subtle Azzigoom!"

"Oo may leave off playing *now*, Sylvie. I can do the uvver tune much better wizout a compliment."

"He means 'without *accompaniment*,'" Sylvie whispered, smiling at my puzzled look: and she pretended to shut up the stops of the organ.

"*The Badgers did not care to talk to Fish:*
They did not dote on Herrings' songs:

They never had experienced the dish
To which that name belongs:
'And oh, to pinch their tails,' (this was their wish,)
'With tongs, yea, tongs, and tongs!'

"*'And are not these the Fish,' the Eldest sighed,*
'Whose Mother dwells beneath the foam?'
'They are *the Fish!' the Second one replied.*
'And they have left their home!'
'Oh wicked Fish,' the Youngest Badger cried,
'To roam, yea, roam, and roam!'

"*Gently the Badgers trotted to the shore—*
The sandy shore that fringed the bay:
Each in his mouth a living Herring bore—
Those aged ones waxed gay:
Clear rang their voices through the ocean's roar,
'Hooray, hooray, hooray!'"

"So they all got safe home again," Bruno said, after waiting a minute to see if *I* had anything to say: he evidently felt that *some* remark ought to be made.

CHAPTER XII

OUTLAND

"The Professor is snoring like anything!" cried Bruno. "Do wake up, you dear old thing!" And he and Sylvie set to work, rolling the heavy head from side to side, as if its connection with the shoulders was a matter of no sort of importance.

And at last the Professor opened his eyes, and sat up, blinking at us with eyes of utter bewilderment. "Would you have the kindness to mention," he said, addressing me with his usual old-fashioned courtesy, "whereabouts we are just now—and *who* we are, beginning with me?"

I thought it best to begin with the children. "This is Sylvie, Sir; and *this* is Bruno."

"Ah, yes! I know *them* well enough!" the old man murmured. "It's *myself* I'm most anxious about."

"Oo're the *Professor!*" Bruno shouted in his ear. "Didn't oo know *that?* Oo've come from *Outland!* And it's *ever* so far away from here!"

The Professor leapt to his feet with the agility of a boy. "Then there's no time to lose!" he exclaimed anxiously. "I'll just ask this guileless peasant, with his brace of buckets that contain (apparently) water, if he'll be so kind as to direct us. Guileless peasant!" he proceeded in a louder voice. "Would you tell us the way to Outland?"

The guileless peasant turned with a sheepish grin. "Hey?" was all he said.

"The—way—to—Outland!" the Professor repeated.

The guileless peasant set down his buckets and considered. "Ah dunnot——"

"I ought to mention," the Professor hastily put in, "that whatever you say will be used in evidence against you."

The guileless peasant instantly resumed his

buckets. "Then ah says nowt!" he answered briskly, and walked away at a great pace.

The children gazed sadly at the rapidly vanishing figure. "He goes very quick!" the Professor said with a sigh. "But I *know* that was the right thing to say. I've studied your English Laws. However, let's ask this next man that's coming. He is *not* guileless, and he is *not* a peasant—but I don't know that either point is of vital importance."

It, was, in fact, the Honourable Eric Lindon, who was strolling leisurely up and .down the road outside the house, enjoying a solitary cigar.

"Might I trouble you, Sir, to tell us the nearest way to Outland!" Oddity as he was, in outward appearance, the Professor was, in that essential nature which no outward disguise could conceal, a thorough gentleman.

And, as such, Eric Lindon accepted him instantly. He took the cigar from his mouth, and delicately shook off the ash, while he considered. "The name sounds strange to me," he said. "I doubt if I can help you."

"It is not *very* far from *Fairyland*," the Professor suggested.

Eric Lindon's eye-brows were slightly raised at these words, and an amused smile which he courteously tried to repress, flitted across his handsome face. "A trifle *cracked!*" he muttered to himself. "But what a jolly old patriarch it is!" Then he turned to the children. "And ca'n't *you* help him, little folk?" he said, with a gentleness of tone that seemed to win their hearts at once. "Surely *you* know all about it?"

> '*How many miles to Babylon?*
> *Three-score miles and ten.*
> *Can I get there by candlelight?*
> *Yes, and back again!*'"

To my surprise, Bruno ran forwards to him, as if he were some old friend of theirs, seized the disengaged hand and hung on to it with both of his own: and there stood this tall dignified officer in the middle of the road, gravely swinging a little boy to and fro, while Sylvie stood ready to push him, exactly as if a real swing had suddenly been provided for their pastime.

"We don't want to get to *Babylon*, oo know!" Bruno explained as he swung.

"And it isn't *candlelight:* it's *daylight!*" Sylvie added, giving the swing a push of extra

vigour, which nearly took the whole machine off its balance.

"How perfectly isochronous!" the Professor exclaimed with enthusiasm. He had his watch in his hand, and was carefully counting Bruno's oscillations. "He measures time quite as accurately as a pendulum!"

"Yet even pendulums," the good-natured young soldier observed, as he carefully released his hand from Bruno's grasp, "are not a joy *for ever!* Come, that's enough for one bout, little man! Next time we meet, you shall have another. Meanwhile you'd better take this old gentleman to Queer Street, Number——"

"*We'll* find it!" cried Bruno eagerly, as they dragged the Professor away.

"We are much indebted to you!" the Professor said, looking over his shoulder.

"Don't mention it!" replied the officer, raising his hat as a parting salute.

"*What* number did you say!" the Professor called from the distance.

The officer made a trumpet of his two hands. "Forty!" he shouted in stentorian tones. "And not *piano*, by any means!" he added to himself. "It's a mad world, my masters, a mad world!" He lit another cigar, and strolled on towards his hotel.

"What a lovely evening!" I said, joining him as he passed me.

"Lovely indeed," he said. "Where did *you* come from? Dropped from the clouds?"

"I'm strolling your way," I said; and no further explanation seemed necessary.

"Have a cigar?"

"Thanks: I'm not a smoker."

"Is there a Lunatic Asylum near here?"

"Not that I know of."

"Thought there might be. Met a lunatic just now. Queer old fish as ever I saw!"

And so, in friendly chat, we took our homeward ways, and wished each other 'good-night' at the door of his hotel.

Left to myself, I felt the 'eerie' feeling rush over me again, and saw standing at the door of Number Forty, the three figures I knew so well.

"Then it's the wrong house?" Bruno was saying.

'No, no! It's the right *house*," the Professor cheerfully replied: "but it's the wrong *street*. *That's* where we've made our mistake! Our best plan, now, will be to——"

It was over. The street was empty. Commonplace life was around me, and the 'eerie' feeling had fled.

CHAPTER XIII

PHLIZZ

On the Tuesday, as I took a long stroll by myself I passed the Station just as the afternoon-train came in sight, and sauntered down the stairs to see it come in. But there was little to gratify my idle curiosity: and, when the train was empty, and the platform clear, I found it was about time to be moving on, if I meant to reach the Hall by five.

As I approached the end of the platform, from which a steep irregular wooden staircase conducted to the upper world, I noticed two passengers, who had evidently arrived by the train, but who, oddly enough, had entirely escaped my notice, though the arrivals had been so few. They were a young woman and a little girl: the former, so far as one could judge by appearances, was a nursemaid, or possibly a nursery governess, in attendance on the child, whose refined face, even more than her dress, distinguished her as of a higher class than her companion.

The child's face was refined, but it was also a worn and sad one, and told a tale (or so I seemed to read it) of much illness and suffering, sweetly and patiently borne. She had a little crutch to help herself along with: and she was now standing, looking wistfully up the long staircase, and apparently waiting till she could muster courage to begin the toilsome ascent.

"May I carry the little girl up the stairs?" I asked.

The servant paused, doubtfully glancing from her charge to me, and then back again to the child. "Would you like it, dear?" she asked her. But no such doubt appeared to cross the child's mind: she lifted her arms eagerly to be taken up. "Please!" was all she said, while a faint smile flickered on the weary little face.

I took her up with scrupulous care, and her little arm was at once clasped trustfully round my neck.

She was a *very* light weight — so light, in fact, that the ridiculous idea crossed my mind that it was rather easier going up, with her in my arms, than it would have been without her: and, when we reached the road above, with its cart-ruts and loose stones—all formidable obstacles for a lame child—I found that I had said "I'd better carry her over this rough place," before I had formed any *mental* connection between its roughness and my gentle little burden. "Indeed, it's troubling you too much, Sir!" the maid exclaimed. "She can walk very well on the flat." But the arm, that was twined about my neck, clung just an atom more closely at the suggestion, and decided me to say "She's no weight, really. I'll carry her a little further. I'm going your way."

The nurse raised no further objection: and the next speaker was a ragged little boy, with bare feet, and a broom over his shoulder, who ran across the road, and pretended to sweep the perfectly dry road in front of us. "Give us a 'ap'ny!" the little urchin pleaded, with a broad grin on his dirty face.

"*Don't* give him a 'ap'ny!" said the little lady in my arms. The *words* sounded harsh: but the *tone* was gentleness itself. "He's an *idle* little boy!" And she laughed a laugh of such silvery sweetness as I had never yet heard from any lips but Sylvie's. To my astonishment, the boy actually *joined* in the laugh, as if there were some subtle sympathy between them, as he ran away down the road and vanished through a gap in the hedge.

But he was back in a few moments, having discarded his broom and provided himself, from some mysterious source, with an exquisite bouquet of flowers. "Buy a posy, buy a posy! Only a 'ap'ny!" he chanted, with the melancholy drawl of a professional beggar.

"*Don't* buy it!" was Her Majesty's edict as she looked down, with a lofty scorn that seemed curiously mixed with tender interest, on the ragged creature at her feet.

But this time I turned rebel, and ignored the royal commands. Such lovely flowers, and of forms so entirely new to me, were not to be abandoned at the bidding of any little maid, however imperious. I bought the bouquet: and the little boy, after popping the halfpenny into his mouth, turned head-over-heels, as if to ascertain whether the human mouth is really adapted to serve as a money-box.

With wonder, that increased every moment, I turned over the flowers, and examined them one by one: there was not a single one among them that I could remember having ever seen before. At last I turned to the nursemaid. "Do these flowers grow wild about here? I never saw——" but the speech died away on my lips. The nursemaid had vanished!

"You can put me down, *now*, if you like," Sylvie quietly remarked.

I obeyed in silence, and could only ask myself "Is this a *dream?*", on finding Sylvie and Bruno walking one on either side of me, and clinging to my hands with the ready confidence of childhood.

"You're larger than when I saw you last!" I began. "Really I think we ought to be introduced again! There's so much of you that I never met before, you know."

"Very well!" Sylvie merrily replied. "This is *Bruno.* It doesn't take long. He's only got one name!"

"There's *another* name to me!" Bruno protested, with a reproachful look at the Mistress of the Ceremonies. "And it's—'*Esquire*'*!*"

"Oh, of course. I forgot," said Sylvie "Bruno—*Esquire!*"

"And did you come here to meet *me*, my children?" I enquired.

"You know I *said* we'd come on Tuesday," Sylvie explained. "Are we the proper size for common children?"

"Quite the right size for *children*," I replied, (adding mentally "though not *common* children, by any means!") "But what became of the nursemaid?"

"It are *gone!*" Bruno solemnly replied.

"Then it wasn't solid, like Sylvie and you?"

"No. Oo couldn't *touch* it, oo know. If oo walked *at* it, oo'd go right froo!"

"I quite expected you'd find it out, once," said Sylvie. "Bruno ran it against a telegraph post, by accident. And it went in two halves. But you were looking the other way."

I felt that I had indeed missed an opportunity: to witness such an event as a nursemaid going 'in two halves' does not occur twice in a life-time!

"When did oo guess it were Sylvie?" Bruno enquired.

"I didn't guess it, till it *was* Sylvie," I said. "But how did you manage the nursemaid?"

"*Bruno* managed it," said Sylvie. "It's called a Phlizz."

"And how do you make a Phlizz, Bruno?"

"The Professor teached me how," said Bruno. "First oo takes a lot of air——"

"Oh, *Bruno!*" Sylvie interposed. "The Professor said you weren't to tell!"

"But who did her *voice?*" I asked.

'Indeed it's troubling you too much, Sir! She can walk very well on the flat."

Bruno laughed merrily as I turned hastily from side to side, looking in all directions for the speaker. "That were *me!*" he gleefully proclaimed, in his own voice.

"She can indeed walk very well on the flat,' I said. "And I think *I* was the Flat."

By this time we were near the Hall. "This is where my friends live," I said. "Will you come in and have some tea with them?"

Bruno gave a little jump of joy: and Sylvie said "Yes, please. You'd like some tea, Bruno, wouldn't you? He hasn't tasted *tea*," she explained to me, "since we left Outland."

"And *that* weren't *good* tea!" said Bruno. "It were so *welly* weak!"

Lady Muriel's smile of welcome could not *quite* conceal the look of surprise with which she regarded my new companions.

I presented them in due form. "This is *Sylvie*, Lady Muriel. And this is *Bruno*."

'Any surname?" she enquired, her eyes twinkling with fun.

"No," I said gravely. "No surname."

She laughed, evidently thinking I said it in fun; and stooped to kiss the children—a salute to which *Bruno* submitted with reluctance: *Sylvie* returned it with interest.

While she supplied the children with tea and cake, I tried to engage her Father, the Earl, in conversation: but he was restless and *distrait*, and we made little progress. At last, by a sudden question, he betrayed the cause of his disquiet.

"*Would* you let me look at those flowers you have in your hand?"

"Willingly!" I said, handing him the bouquet. Botany was, I knew, a favourite study of his: and these flowers were to me so entirely new and mysterious, that I was really curious to see what a botanist would say of them.

They did *not* diminish his disquiet. On the contrary, he became every moment more excited as he turned them over. "*These* are all from Central India!" he said, laying aside part of the bouquet. "They are rare, even there: and I have never seen them in any other part of the world. *These* two are Mexican—*This* one—" (He rose hastily, and carried it to the window, to examine it in a better light, the flush of excitement mounting to his very forehead) "——is, I am nearly sure—but I have a book of Indian Botany here——" He took a volume from the book-shelves, and turned the leaves with trembling fingers. "Yes! Compare it with this picture! It is the exact duplicate! This is the flower of the Upas-tree, which usually grows only in the depths of forests; and the flower fades so quickly after being plucked, that it is scarcely possible to keep its form or colour even so far as the outskirts of the forest! Yet this is in full bloom! *Where* did you get these flowers?" he added with breathless eagerness.

I glanced at Sylvie, who, gravely and silently, laid her finger on her lips, then beckoned to Bruno to follow her, and ran out into the garden; and I found myself in the position of a defendant whose two most important witnesses have been suddenly taken away. "Let me give you the flowers!" I stammered out at last, quite 'at my wit's end' as to how to get out of the difficulty. "You know much more about them than I do!"

"I accept them most gratefully! But you have not yet told me——" the Earl was beginning, when we were interrupted, to my great relief, by the arrival of Eric Lindon.

We made our adieux, and escaped, while the

Earl was still absorbed in examining the mysterious bouquet.

Lady Muriel accompanied us to the door. "You *couldn't* have given my father a more acceptable present!" she said, warmly. "He is so passionately fond of Botany. I'm afraid *I* know nothing of the *theory* of it, but I keep his *Hortus Siccus* in order. I must get some sheets of blotting-paper, and dry these new treasures for him before they fade."

"*That* won't be no good at all!" said Bruno, who was waiting for us in the garden.

"Why won't it?" said I. "You know I *had* to give the flowers, to stop questions."

"Yes, it ca'n't be helped," said Sylvie: "but they *will* be sorry when they find them gone!"

"But how will they go?"

"Well, I don't know *how*. But they *will* go. The nosegay was only a *Phlizz*, you know. Bruno made it up."

The bouquet vanished, as Sylvie had predicted; and when, a day or two afterwards, I once more visited the Hall, I found the Earl and his daughter, with the old housekeeper, out in the garden, examining the fastenings of the drawing-room window.

"We are holding an Inquest," Lady Muriel said, advancing to meet me: "and we admit you as Accessory before the Fact, to tell us all you know about those flowers."

"The Accessory before the Fact declines to answer *any* questions," I gravely replied. "And he reserves his defence."

"Well then, turn Queen's Evidence, please! The flowers have disappeared in the night," she went on, "and we are *quite* sure no one in the house has meddled with them. Somebody must have entered by the window——"

"But the fastenings have not been tampered with," said the Earl.

"It must have been while you were dining, my Lady," said the housekeeper.

"That was it," said the Earl. "The thief must have seen you bring the flowers," turning to me, "and have noticed that you did *not* take them away. And he must have known their great value—they are simply *priceless!*" he exclaimed, in sudden excitement.

"And you never told us how you got them!" said Lady Muriel.

"Some day," I stammered, "I may be free to tell you. Just now, would you excuse me?"

The Earl looked disappointed, but kindly said "Very well, we will ask no questions."

CHAPTER XIV

DINDLEDUMS

"IN that case—" Lady Muriel began, but suddenly started, and turned away to listen. "Don't you hear him?" she said. "He's crying. We must go to him, somehow."

And I said to myself "That's very strange! I quite thought it was *Lady Muriel* talking to me. Why, it's *Sylvie* all the while!"

"Hush! I must think," said Sylvie. "I could go to him, by myself, well enough. But I want *you* to come too."

The door opened, and the Professor looked out. "What's that crying I heard just now?" he asked. "Is it a human animal?"

"It's a boy," Sylvie said.

"I'm afraid you've been teasing him?"

"No, *indeed* I haven't!" Sylvie said, very earnestly. "I *never* tease him!"

"Well, I must ask the Other Professor about it." He went back into the study, and we heard him whispering "small human animal—says she hasn't been teasing him—the kind that's called Boy——"

"Ask her *which* Boy," said a new voice. The Professor came out again.

"*Which* Boy is it that you haven't been teasing?"

Sylvie looked at me with twinkling eyes. "You dear old thing!" she exclaimed, standing on tiptoe to kiss him, while he gravely stooped to receive the salute. "How you *do* puzzle me! Why, there are *several* boys I haven't been teasing!"

The Professor returned to his friend: and this time the voice said "Tell her to bring them here—*all* of them!"

"I ca'n't, and I wo'n't!" Sylvie exclaimed, the moment he reappeared. "It's *Bruno* that's crying: and he's my brother.

The Professor went before us to unlock the

Ivory Door, and locked it behind us. Bruno was standing with his hands over his face, crying bitterly.

"What's the matter, darling?" said Sylvie, with her arms round his neck.

"Hurted mine self *welly* much!" sobbed the poor little fellow.

"I'm *so* sorry, darling! How ever *did* you manage to hurt yourself so?"

"Course I managed it!" said Bruno, laughing through his tears. "Doos oo think nobody else but *oo* can manage things?"

Matters were looking distinctly brighter now Bruno had begun to argue. "Come, let's hear all about it!" I said.

"My foot took it into its head to slip—" Bruno began.

"A foot hasn't got a head!" Sylvie put in, but all in vain.

"I slipted down the bank. And I tripted over a stone. And the stone hurted my foot! And I trod on a Bee. And the Bee stinged my finger!" Poor Bruno sobbed again. The complete list of woes was too much for his feelings. "And it knewed I didn't *mean* to trod on it!" he added, as the climax.

"That Bee should be ashamed of itself!" I said severely, and Sylvie hugged and kissed the wounded hero till all tears were dried.

"My finger's quite unstung now!" said Bruno. "Why does there be stones? Mister Sir, doos oo know?"

"They're good for *something*," I said: "even if we don't know *what*. What's the good of *dandelions*, now?"

"Dindledums?" said Bruno. "Oh, they're ever so pretty! And stones aren't pretty, one bit. Would oo like some dindledums, Mister Sir?"

"Bruno!" Sylvie murmured reproachfully. "You mustn't say 'Mister' and 'Sir,' both at once! Remember what I told you!"

"You telled me I were to say 'Mister' when I spoked *about* him, and I were to say 'Sir' when I spoked *to* him!"

"Well, you're not doing *both*, you know."

"Ah, but I *is* doing bofe, Miss Praticular!" Bruno exclaimed triumphantly. "I wishted to speak *about* the Gemplun—and I wishted to speak *to* the Gemplun. So a course I said 'Mister Sir'!"

"That's all right, Bruno," I said.

"*Course* it's all right!" said Bruno. "Sylvie just knows nuffin at all!"

"There never *was* an impertinenter boy!" said Sylvie, frowning till her bright eyes were nearly invisible.

"And there never was an ignoranter girl!"

retorted Bruno. "Come along and pick some dindledums. *That's all she's fit for!*" he added in a very loud whisper to me.

"But why do you say 'Dindledums,' Bruno? *Dandelions* is the right word."

"It's because he jumps about so," Sylvie said, laughing.

"Yes, that's it," Bruno assented. "Sylvie tells me the words, and then, when I jump about, they get shooken up in my head—till they're all froth!"

I expressed myself as perfectly satisfied with this explanation. "But aren't you going to pick me any dindledums, after all?"

"Course we will!" cried Bruno. "Come along, Sylvie!" And the happy children raced away, bounding over the turf with the fleetness and grace of young antelopes.

"We could only but find *six* dindledums," said Bruno, putting them into my hands, "'cause Sylvie said it were time to go back. And here's a big blackberry for *ooself!* We couldn't only find but *two!*"

"Thank you: it's *very* nice," I said. "And I suppose *you* ate the other, Bruno?"

"No, I didn't," Bruno said, carelessly. "*Aren't* they pretty dindledums, Mister Sir?"

"Yes, very: but what makes you limp so, my child?"

"Mine foot's come *hurted* again!" Bruno mournfully replied. And he sat down on the ground, and began nursing it.

"Shall I go and get you some blackberries, darling?" Sylvie whispered, with her arms round his neck; and she kissed away a tear that was trickling down his cheek.

Bruno brightened up in a moment. "That *are* a good plan!" he exclaimed. "I thinks my foot would come *quite* unhurted, if I eated a blackberry—two or three blackberries—six or seven blackberries——"

Sylvie got up hastily. "I'd better go," she said, aside to me, "before he gets into the double figures!"

"Let me come and help you," I said. "I can reach higher up than you can."

"Yes, please," said Sylvie, putting her hand into mine: and we walked off together.

"Bruno *loves* blackberries," she said, as we paced slowly along by a tall hedge, that looked a promising place for them, "and it was so *sweet* of him to make me eat the only one!"

"Oh, it was *you* that ate it, then? Bruno didn't seem to like to tell me about it."

"No; I saw that," said Sylvie. "He's always afraid of being praised. But he *made* me eat it, really!

CHAPTER XV

FROGS' TREAT

JUST a week after the day when my Fairy-friends first appeared as Children, I found myself taking a farewell-stroll through the wood, in the hope of meeting them once more. I had but to stretch myself on the smooth turf, and the 'eerie' feeling was on me in a moment.

"Put oor ear *welly* low down," said Bruno, "and I'll tell oo a secret! It's the Frogs' Birthday-Treat—and we've lost the Baby!"

"*What* Baby?" I said, quite bewildered by this complicated piece of news.

"The *Queen's* Baby, a course!" said Bruno.

"Titania's Baby. And we's *welly* sorry. Sylvie, she's—oh so sorry!"

"*How* sorry is she?" I asked, mischievously.

"Three-quarters of a yard," Bruno replied with perfect solemnity. "And *I'm* a little sorry too," he added, shutting his eyes so as not to see that he was smiling.

"And what are you doing about the Baby?"

"Well, the *soldiers* are all looking for it—up and down—everywhere."

"The *soldiers?*" I exclaimed.

"Yes, a course!" said Bruno. "When there's no fighting to be done, the soldiers does any little odd jobs, oo know."

I was amused at the idea of its being a 'little odd job' to find the Royal Baby. "But how did you come to lose it?" I asked.

"We put it in a flower," Sylvie, who had just joined us, explained with her eyes full of tears. "Only we ca'n't remember *which!*"

"She says *us* put it in a flower," Bruno interrupted, "'cause she doosn't want *I* to get punished. But it were really *me* what put it there. *Sylvie* were picking Dindledums."

"You shouldn't say '*us* put it in a flower,'" Sylvie very gravely remarked.

"Well, *hus*, then," said Bruno. "I never *can* remember those horrid H's!"

"Let me help you to look for it," I said. So Sylvie and I made a 'voyage of discovery' among all the flowers; but there was no Baby to be seen.

"What's become of Bruno?' I said, when we had completed our tour.

"He's down in the ditch there," said Sylvie, "amusing a young Frog."

I went down on my hands and knees to look for him, for I felt very curious to know how young Frogs *ought* to be amused. After a minute's search, I found him sitting at the edge of the ditch, by the side of the little Frog, and looking rather disconsolate.

"How are you getting on, Bruno?" I said, nodding to him as he looked up.

"Ca'n't amuse it no more," Bruno answered, very dolefully, "'cause it won't say what it would like to do next! I've showed it all the duck-weeds—and a live caddis-worm—but it won't say nuffin! What—would oo—like?" he shouted into the ear of the Frog: but the little creature sat quite still, and took no notice of him. "It's deaf, I think!" Bruno said, turning away with a sigh. "And it's time to get the Theatre ready."

"Who are the audience to be?"

"Only but Frogs," said Bruno. "But they haven't comed yet. They wants to be drove up, like sheep."

"Would it save time," I suggested, "if *I* were to walk round with Sylvie, and drive up the Frogs, while *you* get the Theatre ready?"

"That *are* a good plan!" cried Bruno. "But where *are* Sylvie?"

"I'm here!" said Sylvie, peeping over the edge of the bank. "I was just watching two Frogs that were having a race."

"Which won it?" Bruno eagerly enquired.

Sylvie was puzzled. "He *does* ask such hard questions!" she confided to me.

"And what's to happen in the Theatre?" I asked.

"First they have their Birthday-Feast," Sylvie said: "then Bruno does some Bits of Shakespeare; then he tells them a Story."

"I should think the Frogs like the Feast best. Don't they?"

"Well, there's generally very few of them that get any. They *will* keep their mouths shut so tight! And it's just as well they *do*," she added, "because Bruno likes to cook it himself: and he cooks *very* queerly. Now they're all in. Would you just help me to put them with their heads the right way?"

We soon managed this part of the business, though the Frogs kept up a most discontented croaking all the time.

"What *are* they saying?" I asked Sylvie.

"They're saying 'Fork! Fork!' It's very silly of them! You're not going to *have* forks!" she announced with some severity. "Those that want any Feast have just got to open their mouths, and Bruno'll put some of it in!"

At this moment Bruno appeared, wearing a little white apron to show that he was a Cook, and carrying a tureen full of very queer-looking soup. I watched very carefully as he moved about among the Frogs; but I could not see that *any* of them opened their mouths to be fed—except one very young one, and I'm nearly sure it did it accidentally, in yawning. However Bruno instantly put a large spoonful of soup into its mouth, and the poor little thing coughed violently for some time.

So Sylvie and I had to share the soup between us, and to *pretend* to enjoy it, for it certainly was *very* queerly cooked.

I only ventured to take *one* spoonful of it ("Sylvie's Summer-Soup," Bruno said it was), and must candidly confess that it was not *at all* nice; and I could not feel surprised that so many of the guests had kept their mouths shut up tight.

"What's the soup *made* of, Bruno?" said Sylvie, who had put a spoonful of it to her lips, and was making a wry face over it.

And Bruno's answer was anything but encouraging. "Bits of things!"

The entertainment was to conclude with "Bits of Shakespeare," as Sylvie expressed it, which were all to be done by Bruno, Sylvie being fully engaged in making the Frogs keep their heads towards the stage: after which Bruno was to appear in his real character, and tell them a Story of his own invention.

"Will the Story have a Moral to it?" I asked Sylvie, while Bruno was away behind the hedge, dressing for the first 'Bit.'

"I *think* so," Sylvie replied doubtfully. "There generally *is* a Moral, only he puts it in too soon."

"And will he *say* all the Bits of Shakespeare?"

"No, he'll only *act* them," said Sylvie. "He knows hardly any of the words. When I see what he's dressed like, I've to tell the Frogs what character it is. They're always in such a hurry to guess! Don't you hear them all saying 'What? What?'" And so indeed they were: it had only sounded like croaking, till Sylvie explained it, but I could now make out the "Wawt? Wawt?" quite distinctly.

"But why do they try to guess it before they see it?"

"I don't know," Sylvie said: "but they always *do*. Sometimes they begin guessing weeks and weeks before the day!"

However, the chorus of guessing was cut short by Bruno, who suddenly rushed on from behind the scenes, and took a flying leap down among the Frogs, to re-arrange them.

For the oldest and fattest Frog—who had never been properly arranged so that he could see the stage, and so had no idea what was going on—was getting restless, and had upset several of the Frogs, and turned others round with their heads the wrong way. And it was no good at all, Bruno said, to do a 'Bit' of Shakespeare when there was nobody to look at it (you see he didn't count *me* as anybody). So he set to work with a stick, stirring them up, very much as you would stir up tea in a cup, till most of them had at least *one* great stupid eye gazing at the stage.

"*Oo* must come and sit among them, Sylvie," he said in despair, "I've put these two side-by-side, with their noses the same way, ever so many times, but they *do* squarrel so!"

So Sylvie took her place as 'Mistress of the Ceremonies,' and Bruno vanished again behind the scenes, to dress for the first 'Bit.'

"Hamlet!" was suddenly proclaimed, in the clear sweet tones I knew so well. The croaking all ceased in a moment, and I turned to the stage, in some curiosity to see what Bruno's ideas were as to the behaviour of Shakespeare's greatest Character.

According to this eminent interpreter of the Drama, Hamlet wore a short black cloak (which he chiefly used for muffling up his face, as if he suffered a good deal from toothache), and turned out his toes very much as he walked. "To be or not to be!" Hamlet remarked in a cheerful tone, and then turned head-over-heels several times, his cloak dropping off in the performance.

I felt a little disappointed: Bruno's conception of the part seemed so wanting in dignity. "Won't he say any more of the speech?" I whispered to Sylvie.

"I *think* not," Sylvie whispered in reply. "He generally turns head-over-heels when he doesn't know any more words."

Bruno had meanwhile settled the question by disappearing from the stage; and the Frogs instantly began enquiring the name of the next Character.

"You'll know directly!" cried Sylvie, as she adjusted two or three young Frogs that had struggled round with their backs to the stage. "Macbeth!" she added, as Bruno re-appeared.

Macbeth had something twisted round him, that went over one shoulder and under the other arm, and was meant, I believe, for a Scotch plaid. He had a thorn in his hand, which he held out at arm's length, as if he were a little afraid of it. "Is this a *dagger?*" Macbeth enquired, in a puzzled sort of tone: and instantly a chorus of "Thorn! Thorn!" arose from the Frogs (I had quite learned to understand their croaking by this time).

"It's a *dagger!*" Sylvie proclaimed in a peremptory tone. "Hold your tongues!" And the croaking ceased at once.

Shakespeare has not told us, so far as I know, that Macbeth had any such eccentric habit as turning head-over-heels in private life: but Bruno evidently considered it quite an essential part of the character, and left the stage in a series of somersaults. However, he was back again in a few moments, having tucked under his chin the end of a tuft of wool (probably left on the thorn by a wandering sheep), which made a magnificent beard, that reached nearly down to his feet.

"Shylock!" Sylvie proclaimed. "No, I beg your pardon!" she hastily corrected herself, "King Lear! I hadn't noticed the crown." (Bruno had very cleverly provided one, which fitted him exactly, by cutting out the centre of a dandelion to make room for his head.)

King Lear folded his arms (to the imminent peril of his beard) and said, in a mild explanatory tone, "Ay, every *inch* a king!" and then paused, as if to consider how this could best be proved. And here, with all possible deference

Harry Furniss

to Bruno as a Shakespearian critic, I *must* express my opinion that the poet did *not* mean his three great tragic heroes to be so strangely alike in their personal habits; nor do I believe that he would have accepted the faculty of turning head-over-heels as any proof at all of royal descent. Yet it appeared that King Lear, after deep meditation, could think of no other argument by which to prove his kingship: and as this was the last of the 'Bits' of Shakespeare ("We never do more than *three*," Sylvie explained in a whisper), Bruno gave the audience quite a long series of somersaults before he finally retired, leaving the enraptured Frogs all crying out "More! More!" which I suppose was their way of encoring a performance. But Bruno wouldn't appear again, till the proper time came for telling the Story.

When he appeared at last in his *real* character, I noticed a remarkable change in his behaviour. He tried no more somersaults. It was clearly his opinion that, however suitable the habit of turning head-over-heels might be to such petty individuals as Hamlet and King Lear, it would never do for *Bruno* to sacrifice his dignity to such an extent. But it was equally clear that he did not feel entirely at his ease, standing all alone on the stage, with no costume to disguise him: and though he began, several times, "There were a Mouse—," he kept glancing up and down, and on all sides, as if in search of more comfortable quarters from which to tell the Story. Standing on one side of the stage, and partly overshadowing it, was a tall foxglove, which seemed, as the evening breeze gently swayed it hither and thither, to offer exactly the sort of accommodation that the orator desired. Having once decided on his quarters, it needed only a second or two for him to run up the stem like a tiny squirrel, and to seat himself astride on the topmost bend, where the fairy-bells clustered most closely, and from whence he could look down on his audience from such a height that all shyness vanished, and he began his Story merrily.

"Once there were a Mouse and a Crocodile and a Man and a Goat and a Lion." I had never heard the 'dramatis personæ' tumbled into a story with such profusion and in such reckless haste; and it fairly took my breath away. Even Sylvie gave a little gasp, and allowed three of the Frogs, who seemed to be getting tired of the entertainment, to hop away into the ditch, without attempting to stop them.

"And the Mouse found a Shoe, and it thought it were a Mouse-trap. So it got right in, and it stayed in ever so long."

"Why did it *stay* in?" said Sylvie. Her function seemed to be much the same as that of the Chorus in a Greek Play: she had to encourage the orator, and draw him out, by a series of intelligent questions.

"'Cause it thought it couldn't get out again," Bruno explained. "It were a clever mouse. It knew it couldn't get out of traps!"

"But why did it go in at all?" said Sylvie.

"—and it jamp, and it jamp," Bruno proceeded, ignoring this question, "and at last it got right out again. And it looked at the mark in the Shoe. And the Man's name were in it. So it knew it wasn't its own Shoe."

"Had it thought it *was?*" said Sylvie.

"Why, didn't I tell oo it thought it were a *Mouse-trap?*" the indignant orator replied.

"Please, Mister Sir, will oo make Sylvie attend?" Sylvie was silenced, and was all attention: in fact, she and I were most of the audience now, as the Frogs kept hopping away, and there were very few of them left.

"So the Mouse gave the Man his Shoe. And the Man were welly glad, 'cause he hadn't got but one Shoe, and he were hopping to get the other."

Here I ventured on a question. "Do you mean 'hopping,' or 'hoping'?"

"Bofe," said Bruno. "And the Man took the Goat out of the Sack." ("We haven't heard of the *sack* before," I said. "Nor you won't hear of it again," said Bruno.) "And he said to the Goat, 'Oo will walk about here till I comes back.' And he went and he tumbled into a deep hole. And the Goat walked round and round. And it walked under the Tree. And it wug its tail. And it looked up in the Tree. And it sang a sad little Song. Oo never heard such a sad little Song!"

"Can you sing it, Bruno?" I asked.

"Iss, I can," Bruno readily replied. "And I sa'n't. It would make Sylvie cry——"

"It wouldn't!" Sylvie interrupted in great indignation. "And I don't believe the Goat sang it at all!"

"It did, though!" said Bruno. "It singed it right froo. I *sawed* it singing with its long beard——"

"It couldn't sing with its *beard*," I said, hoping to puzzle the little fellow: "a beard isn't a *voice*."

"Well then, *oo* couldn't walk with Sylvie!" Bruno cried triumphantly. "Sylvie isn't a *foot!*"

I thought I had better follow Sylvie's example, and be silent for a while. Bruno was too sharp for us.

"And when it had singed all the Song, it ran away—for to get along to look for the Man, oo know. And the Crocodile got along after it—for to bite it, oo know. And the Mouse got along after the Crocodile."

"Wasn't the Crocodile *running?*" Sylvie enquired. She appealed to me. "Crocodiles do run, don't they?"

I suggested "crawling" as the proper word.

"He wasn't running," said Bruno, "and he

wasn't crawling. He went struggling along like a portmanteau. And he held his chin ever so high in the air——"

"What did he do *that* for?" said Sylvie.

"'cause he hadn't got a toofache!" said Bruno. "Ca'n't oo make out *nuffin* wizout I 'splain it? Why, if he'd had a toofache, a course he'd have held his head down—like this—and he'd have put a lot of warm blankets round it!"

"If he'd *had* any blankets!" Sylvie argued.

"Course he *had* blankets!" retorted her brother. "Doos oo think Crocodiles goes walks wizout blankets? And he frowned with his eyebrows. And the Goat was welly flightened at his eyebrows!"

"I'd never be afraid of *eyebrows!*" exclaimed Sylvie.

"I should think oo *would*, though, if they'd got a Crocodile fastened to them, like these had! And so the Man jamp, and he jamp and at last he got right out of the hole."

Sylvie gave another little gasp: this rapid dodging about among the characters of the Story had taken away her breath.

"And he runned away—for to look for the Goat, oo know. And he heard the Lion grunting——"

"Lions don't grunt," said Sylvie.

"This one did," said Bruno. "And its mouth were like a large cupboard. And it had plenty of room in its mouth. And the Lion runned after the Man—for to eat him, oo know. And the Mouse runned after the Lion."

"But the Mouse was running after the *Crocodile*," I said: "he couldn't run after *both!*"

Bruno sighed over the density of his audience, but explained very patiently. "He *did* runned after *bofe:* 'cause they went the same way! And first he caught the Crocodile, and then he didn't catch the Lion. And when he'd caught the Crocodile, what doos oo think he did—'cause he'd got pincers in his pocket?"

"I ca'n't guess," said Sylvie.

"Nobody couldn't guess it!" Bruno cried in high glee. "Why, he wrenched out that Crocodile's toof!"

"*Which* tooth?" I ventured to ask.

But Bruno was not to be puzzled. "The

toof he were going to bite the Goat with, a course!"

"He couldn't be sure about that," I argued "unless he wrenched out *all* its teeth."

Bruno laughed merrily, and half sang, as he swung himself backwards and forwards, "He did—wrenched—out—*all* its teef!"

"Why did the Crocodile wait to have them wrenched out?" said Sylvie.

"It had to wait," said Bruno.

I ventured on another question. "But what became of the Man who said 'You may wait here till I come back'?"

"He didn't say 'Oo *may*,'" Bruno explained. "He said, 'Oo *will*.' Just like Sylvie says to me 'Oo will do oor lessons till twelve o'clock.' Oh, I *wiss*," he added with a little sigh, "I *wiss* Sylvie would say 'Oo *may* do oor lessons'!"

This was a dangerous subject for discussion, Sylvie seemed to think. She returned to the Story. "But what became of the Man?"

"Well, the Lion springed at him. But it came so slow, it were three weeks in the air——"

"Did the Man wait for it all that time?" I said.

"Course he didn't!" Bruno replied, gliding head first down the stem of the fox-glove, for the Story was evidently close to its end. "He sold his house, and he packed up his things, while the Lion were coming. And he went and he lived in another town. So the Lion ate the wrong man."

This was evidently the Moral: so Sylvie made her final proclamation to the Frogs. "The Story's finished! And whatever is to be *learned* from it," she added, aside to me, "I'm sure *I* don't know!"

I did not feel *quite* clear about it myself, so made no suggestion: but the Frogs seemed quite content, Moral or no Moral, and merely raised a husky chorus of "Off! Off!" as they hopped away.

CHAPTER XVI

LESSONS

To while away the time, I strolled, one afternoon, into Kensington Gardens, and, wandering aimlessly along any path that presented itself, when I chanced to notice a small creature, moving among the grass that fringed the path, that did not seem to be an insect, or a frog, or any other living thing that I could think of. Cautiously kneeling down, and making an *ex tempore* cage of my two hands, I imprisoned the little wanderer, and felt a sudden thrill of surprise and delight on discovering that my prisoner was no other than *Bruno* himself!

Bruno took the matter *very* coolly, and, when I had replaced him on the ground, where he would be within easy conversational distance, he began talking, just as if it were only a few minutes since last we had met.

"Doos oo know what the *Rule* is," he enquired, "when oo catches a Fairy, withouten its having tolded oo where it was?" (Bruno's notions of English Grammar had certainly *not* improved since our last meeting.)

"No," I said. "I didn't know there was any Rule about it."

"I *think* oo've got a right to *eat* me," said the little fellow, looking up into my face with a winning smile. "But I'm not pruffickly sure. Oo'd better not do it wizout asking."

It did indeed seem reasonable not to take so irrevocable a step as *that*, without due enquiry. "I'll certainly *ask* about it, first," I said. "Besides, I don't know yet whether you would be *worth* eating!"

"I guess I'm *deliciously* good to eat," Bruno remarked in a satisfied tone, as if it were something to be rather proud of.

"And what are you doing here, Bruno?"

"*That's* not my name!" said my cunning little friend. "Don't oo know my name's 'Oh

Bruno!'? That's what Sylvie always calls me, when I says mine lessons."

"Well then, what are you doing here, oh Bruno?"

"Doing mine lessons, a-course!" With that roguish twinkle in his eye, that always came when he knew he was talking nonsense.

"Oh, *that's* the way you do your lessons, is it? And do you remember them well?"

"Always can 'member *mine* lessons," said Bruno. "It's *Sylvie's* lessons that's so *dreffully* hard to 'member!" He frowned as if in agonies of thought, and tapped his forehead with his knuckles. "I *ca'n't* think enough to understand them!" he said despairingly. "It wants *double* thinking, I believe!"

"But where's Sylvie gone?"

"That's just what *I* want to know!" said Bruno disconsolately. "What ever's the good of setting me lessons, when she isn't here to 'splain the hard bits?"

"*I'll* find her for you!" I volunteered; and, getting up, I wandered round the tree under whose shade I had been reclining, looking on all sides for Sylvie. In another minute I *again* noticed some strange thing moving among the grass, and, kneeling down, was immediately confronted with Sylvie's innocent face, lighted up with a joyful surprise at seeing me, and was accosted, in the sweet voice I knew so well, with what seemed to be the *end* of a sentence whose beginning I had failed to catch.

"——and I think he ought to have *finished* them by this time. So I'm going back to him. Will you come too? It's only just round at the other side of this tree."

To find Bruno's *lessons* was easy enough: they appeared to be neatly written out on large smooth ivy-leaves, which were scattered in some confusion over a little patch of ground where the grass had been worn away; but the pale student, who ought by rights to have been bending over them, was nowhere to be seen: we looked in all directions, for some time, in vain; but at last Sylvie's sharp eyes detected him, swinging on a tendril of ivy, and Sylvie's stern voice commanded his instant return to *terra firma* and to the business of Life.

"Pleasure first and business afterwards"

seemed to be the motto of these tiny folk, so many hugs and kisses had to be interchanged before anything else could be done.

"Now, Bruno," Sylvie said reproachfully,

"didn't I tell you you were to go on with your lessons, unless you heard to the contrary?"

"But I *did* heard to the contrary!" Bruno insisted, with a mischievous twinkle in his eye.

"*What* did you hear, you wicked boy?"

"It were a sort of noise in the air," said Bruno: "a sort of a scrambling noise. Didn't *oo* hear it, Mister Sir?"

"Well, anyhow, you needn't go to *sleep* over them, you lazy-lazy!" For Bruno had curled himself up, on the largest 'lesson,' and was arranging another as a pillow.

"I *wasn't* asleep!" said Bruno, in a deeply-injured tone. "When I shuts mine eyes, it's to show that I'm *awake!*"

"Well, how much have you learned, then?"

"I've learned a little tiny bit," said Bruno, modestly, being evidently afraid of overstating his achievement. "*Ca'n't* learn no more!"

"Oh Bruno! You know you *can*, if you like."

"Course I can, if I *like*," the pale student replied; "but I ca'n't if I *don't* like!"

Sylvie had a way—which I could not too highly admire—of evading Bruno's logical perplexities by suddenly striking into a new line of thought; and this masterly stratagem she now adopted.

"Well, I must say *one* thing——"

"Did oo know, Mister Sir," Bruno thoughtfully remarked, "that Sylvie ca'n't count? Whenever she says 'I must say *one* thing,' I *know* quite well she'll say *two* things! And she always doos."

"Two heads are better than one, Bruno," I said, but with no very distinct idea as to what I meant by it.

"I shouldn't mind having two *heads*," Bruno said softly to himself: "one head to eat mine dinner, and one head to argue wiz Sylvie—doos oo think oo'd look prettier if oo'd got *two* heads, Mister Sir?"

The case did not, I assured him, admit of a doubt.

"The reason why Sylvie's so cross——" Bruno went on very seriously, almost sadly.

Sylvie's eyes grew large and round with surprise at this new line of enquiry—her rosy face being perfectly radiant with good humour. But she said nothing.

"Wouldn't it be better to tell me after the lessons are over?" I suggested.

"Very well," Bruno said with a resigned air: "only she wo'n't be cross then."

"There's only three lessons to do," said Sylvie. "Spelling, and Geography, and Singing."

"Not *Arithmetic?*" I said.

"No, he hasn't a head for Arithmetic——"

"Course I haven't!" said Bruno. "Mine head's for *hair*. I haven't got a *lot* of heads!"

"—and he ca'n't learn his Multiplication-table——"

"I like *History* ever so much better," Bruno remarked. "Oo has to *repeat* that Muddlecome table——"

"Well, and you have to repeat——"

"No, oo hasn't!" Bruno interrupted. "History repeats itself. The Professor said so!"

Sylvie was arranging some letters on a board—E—V—I—L. "Now, Bruno," she said, "what does *that* spell?"

Bruno looked at it, in solemn silence, for a minute. "I knows what it *doesn't* spell!" he said at last.

"That's no good," said Sylvie. "What *does* it spell?"

Bruno took another look at the mysterious letters. "Why, it's 'LIVE,' backwards!" he exclaimed. (I thought it was, indeed.)

"How *did* you manage to see that?" said Sylvie.

"I just twiddled my eyes," said Bruno, "and then I saw it directly. Now may I sing the King-fisher Song?"

"Geography next," said Sylvie. "Don't you know the Rules?"

"I thinks there oughtn't to be such a lot of Rules, Sylvie! I thinks——"

"Yes, there *ought* to be such a lot of Rules, you wicked, wicked boy! And how dare you *think* at all about it? And shut up that mouth directly!"

So, as 'that mouth' didn't seem inclined to shut up of itself, Sylvie shut it for him—with both hands—and sealed it with a kiss, just as you would fasten up a letter.

"Now that Bruno is fastened up from talking," she went on, turning to me, "I'll show you the Map he does his lessons on."

And there it was, a large Map of the World, spread out on the ground. It was so large that Bruno had to crawl about on it, to point out the places named in the 'King-fisher Lesson.'

"When a King-fisher sees a Lady-bird flying away, he says '*Ceylon*, if you *Candia!*' And when he catches it, he says 'Come to *Media!* And if you're *Hungary* or thirsty, I'll give you some *Nubia!*' When he takes it in his claws, he says '*Europe!*' When he puts it into his beak, he says '*India!*' When he's swallowed it, he says '*Eton!*' That's all."

"That's *quite* perfect," said Sylvie. "Now you may sing the King-fisher Song."

"Will *oo* sing the chorus?" Bruno said to me.

I was just beginning to say "I'm afraid I don't know the *words*," when Sylvie silently turned the map over, and I found the words were all written on the back. In one respect it was a *very* peculiar song: the chorus to each verse came in the *middle*, instead of at the *end* of it. However, the tune was so easy that I soon picked it up, and managed the chorus as well, perhaps, as it is possible for *one* person to manage such a thing. It was in vain that I signed to Sylvie to help me: she only smiled sweetly and shook her head.

"*King Fisher courted Lady Bird*——
Sing Beans, sing Bones, sing Butterflies!
'*Find me my match,' he said,*
'*With such a noble head*——
With such a beard, as white as curd——
With such expressive eyes!'

"'*Yet pins have heads,' said Lady Bird*——
Sing Prunes, sing Prawns, sing Primrose-Hill!
'*And, where you stick them in,*
They stay, and thus a pin
Is very much to be preferred
To one that's never still!'

"'*Oysters have beards,' said Lady Bird*——
Sing Flies, sing Frogs, sing Fiddle-strings!
'*I love them, for I know*
They *never chatter so:*
They would not say one single word——
Not if you crowned them Kings!'

"'*Needles have eyes,*' *said Lady Bird*——
Sing Cats, sing Corks, sing Cowslip-tea!
'*And they are sharp—just what*
Your Majesty is not:
So get you gone—'tis too absurd
To come a-courting me!'"

"So he went away," Bruno added as a kind of postscript, when the last note of the song had died away. "Just like he always did."

"Oh, my *dear* Bruno!" Sylvie exclaimed, with her hands over her ears. "You shouldn't say 'like': you should say '*what.*'"

To which Bruno replied, doggedly, "I only says 'what!' when oo doosn't speak loud, so as I can hear oo."

"Where did he go to?" I asked, hoping to prevent an argument.

"He went more far than he'd never been before," said Bruno.

"You should never say 'more far,'" Sylvie corrected him: "you should say '*farther.*'"

"Then *oo* shouldn't say 'more broth,' when we're at dinner," Bruno retorted: "oo should say '*brother*'*!*"

This time Sylvie evaded an argument by turning away, and beginning to roll up the Map. "Lessons are over!" she proclaimed in her sweetest tones.

"And has there been no *crying* over them?" I enquired. "Little boys *always* cry over their lessons, don't they?"

"I never cries after twelve o'clock," said Bruno: "'cause then it's getting so near to dinner-time."

"Sometimes, in the morning," Sylvie said in a low voice; "when it's Geography-day, and when he's been disobe——"

"*What* a fellow you are to talk, Sylvie!" Bruno hastily interposed. "Doos oo think the world was *made* for oo to talk in?"

"Why, where would you *have* me talk, then?" Sylvie said, evidently quite ready for an argument.

But Bruno answered resolutely. "I'm not going to argue about it, 'cause it's getting late, and there wo'n't be time—but oo's as 'ong as ever oo can be!" And he rubbed the back of his hand across his eyes, in which tears were beginning to glitter.

Sylvie's eyes filled with tears in a moment. "I didn't mean it, Bruno, *darling!*" she whispered; and the rest of the argument was lost 'amid the tangles of Neæra's hair,' while the two disputants hugged and kissed each other.

But this new form of argument was brought to a sudden end by a flash of lightning, which was closely followed by a peal of thunder, and by a torrent of rain-drops, which came hissing and spitting, almost like live creatures, through the leaves of the tree that sheltered us.

"Why, it's raining cats and dogs!" I said.

"And all the *dogs* has come down *first*," said Bruno: "there's nothing but *cats* coming down now!"

CHAPTER XVII

STOP THIEF !

"WELL, we must get on, now, as quick as we can," I said. "If only I knew the best way to Hunter's farm!"

"They'll be sure to know in this cottage," said Sylvie.

"Yes, I suppose they will. Bruno, would you run in and ask?"

Sylvie stopped him, laughingly, as he ran off. "Wait a minute," she said. "I must make you *visible* first, you know."

"And *audible* too, I suppose!" I said, as she took the jewel that hung round her neck, and waved it over his head, and touched his eyes and lips with it.

"Yes," said Sylvie: "and *once*, do you know, I made him *audible*, and forgot to make him *visible!* And he went to buy some sweeties in a shop. And the man *was* so frightened! A voice seemed to come out of the air, 'Please, I want two ounces of barley-sugar drops!' And a shilling came *bang* down upon the counter! And the man said 'I ca'n't *see* you!' And Bruno said 'It doosn't sinnify seeing *me*, so long as oo can see the *shilling!*' But the man said he never sold barley-sugar drops to people he couldn't *see*. So we had to—*Now*, Bruno, you're ready!" And away he trotted.

Sylvie spent the time, while we were waiting for him, in making *herself* visible also. "It's rather awkward, you know," she explained to me, "when we meet people, and they can see *one* of us, and ca'n't see the *other!*"

In a minute or two Bruno returned, looking rather disconsolate. "He'd got friends with him, and he were *cross!*" he said. "He asked me who I were. And I said 'I'm Bruno: who is *these* peoples?'" And he said 'One's my half-brother, and t'other's my half-sister: and I don't want no more company! Go along with yer!' And I said 'I ca'n't go along *wizout* mine self!' And said "Oo shouldn't have *bits* of peoples lying about like that! It's welly untidy!' And he said 'Oh, don't talk to *me!* And he pushted me outside! And he shutted the door!"

"And you never asked where Hunter's farm was?" queried Sylvie.

"Hadn't room for any questions," said Bruno. "The room were so crowded."

"Three people *couldn't* crowd a room," said Sylvie.

"They *did*, though," Bruno persisted. "*He* crowded it most. He's such a welly *thick* man—so as oo couldn't knock him down."

I failed to see the drift of Bruno's argument. "Surely *anybody* could be knocked down," I said: "thick or thin wouldn't matter."

"Oo couldn't knock *him* down," said Bruno. "He's more wider than he's high: so, when he's lying down, he's more higher than when he's standing: so a-course oo couldn't knock him *down!*"

"Here's another cottage," I said: "*I'll* ask the way, *this* time."

"Perhaps you can tell me where Hunter's farm is?" I said to the man.

"I can *that*, Sir!" he replied with a smile. "I'm John Hunter hissel, at your sarvice. It's nobbut half a mile further—the only house in sight, when you get round bend o' the road yonder. You'll find my good woman within, if so be you've business wi' *her*. Or mebbe I'll do as well?"

"Thanks," I said. "I want to order some milk. Perhaps I had better arrange it with your wife?"

"Aye," said the man. "*She* minds all *that*. Good day t'ye, Master—and to your bonnie childer, as well!" And he trudged on.

"He should have said '*child*,' not '*childer*'," said Bruno. "Sylvie's not a *childer!*"

"He meant *both* of us," said Sylvie.

"No, he didn't!" Bruno persisted, "'cause he said 'bonnie', oo know!"

"Well, at any rate he *looked* at us both," Sylvie maintained.

"Well, then he *must* have seen we're not *both* bonnie!" Bruno retorted. "A-*course* I'm much uglier than *oo!* Didn't he mean *Sylvie*,

Mister Sir?" he shouted over his shoulder, as he ran off.

But there was no use in replying, as he had already vanished round the bend of the road. When we overtook him he was climbing a gate, and was gazing earnestly into the field, where a horse, a cow, and a kid were browsing amicably together. "For its father, a *Horse*," he murmured to himself. "For its mother, a *Cow*. For their dear little child, a *little* Goat, is the most curiousest thing I ever seen in my world!"

"That *must* be Hunter's farm!" said Sylvie, pointing to a house on the brow of the hill, led up to by a cart-road. "There's no other farm in sight, *this* way; and you *said* we must be nearly there by this time."

I had *thought* it, while Bruno was climbing the gate, but I couldn't remember having *said* it. However, Sylvie was evidently in the right. "Get down, Bruno," I said, "and open the gate for us."

"It's a good thing we's with oo, *isn't* it, Mister Sir?" said Bruno, as we entered the field. "That big dog might have bited oo, if oo'd been alone! Oo needn't be *flightened* of it!" he whispered, clinging tight to my hand to encourage me. "It aren't fierce!"

"Fierce!" Sylvie scornfully echoed, as the dog—a magnificent Newfoundland—that had come galloping down the field to meet us, began curveting round us, in gambols full of graceful beauty, and welcoming us with short joyful barks. "Fierce! Why, it's as gentle as a lamb! It's—why, Bruno, don't you know it? It's——"

"So it *are!*" cried Bruno, rushing forwards and throwing his arms round its neck. "Oh, you *dear* dog!" And it seemed as if the two children would never have done hugging and stroking it.

"And how *ever* did he get *here?*" said Bruno. "Ask him, Sylvie. I doosn't know how."

And then began an eager talk in Doggee, which of course was lost upon *me;* and I could only *guess*, when the beautiful creature, with a sly glance at me, whispered something in Sylvie's ear, that *I* was now the subject of conversation. Sylvie looked round laughingly.

"He asked me who you are," she explained.

"And I said 'He's our *friend.*' And he said 'What's his name?' And I said 'It's *Mister Sir.*' And he said 'Bosh!'"

"What is 'Bosh!' in Doggee?" I enquired.

"It's the same as in English," said Sylvie. "Only, when a *dog* says it, it's a sort of a whisper, that's half a *cough* and half a *bark.* Nero, say '*Bosh!*'"

And Nero, who had now begun gamboling round us again, said "*Bosh!*" several times; and I found that Sylvie's description of the sound was perfectly accurate.

"I wonder what's behind this long wall?" I said, as we walked on.

"It's the *Orchard,*" Sylvie replied, after a consultation with Nero. "See, there's a boy getting down off the wall, at that far corner. And now he's running away across the field. I do believe he's been stealing the apples!"

Bruno set off after him, but returned to us in a few moments, as he had evidently no chance of overtaking the young rascal.

"I couldn't catch him!" he said. "I wiss I'd started a little sooner. His pockets *was* full of apples!"

The Dog-King looked up at Sylvie, and said something in Doggee.

"Why, of *course* you can!" Sylvie exclaimed. "How stupid not to think of it! *Nero*'ll hold him for us, Bruno! But I'd better make him invisible, first." And she hastily got out the Magic Jewel, and began waving it over Nero's head, and down along his back.

"That'll do!" cried Bruno, impatiently. "After him, good Doggie!"

"Oh, Bruno!" Sylvie exclaimed reproachfully. "You shouldn't have sent him off so quick! I hadn't done the tail!"

Meanwhile Nero was coursing like a greyhound down the field: so at least I concluded from all *I* could see of him—the long feathery tail, which floated like a meteor through the air—and in a very few seconds he had come up with the little thief.

"He's got him safe, by one foot!" cried Sylvie, who was eagerly watching the chase. "Now there's no hurry, Bruno!"

So we walked, quite leisurely, down the field, to where the frightened lad stood. A more curious sight I had seldom seen, in all

my 'eerie' experiences. Every bit of him was in violent action, except the left foot, which was apparently glued to the ground—there being nothing visibly holding it: while, at some little distance, the long feathery tail was waving gracefully from side to side, showing that Nero, at least, regarded the whole affair as nothing but a magnificent game of play.

"What's the matter with you?" I said, as gravely as I could.

"Got the crahmp in me ahnkle!" the thief groaned in reply. "An' me fut's gone to sleep!" And he began to blubber aloud.

"Now, look here!" Bruno said in a commanding tone, getting in front of him. "Oo've got to give up those apples!"

The lad glanced at me, but didn't seem to reckon *my* interference as worth anything. Then he glanced at Sylvie: *she* clearly didn't count for very much, either. Then he took courage. "It'll take a better man than any of *yer* to get 'em!" he retorted defiantly.

Sylvie stooped and patted the invisible Nero. "A *little* tighter!" she whispered. And a sharp yell from the ragged boy showed how promptly the Dog-King had taken the hint.

"What's the matter *now!*" I said. "Is your ankle worse?"

"And it'll get worse, and worse, and worse," Bruno solemnly assured him, "till oo gives up those apples!"

Apparently the thief was convinced of this at last, and he sulkily began emptying his pockets of the apples. The children watched from a little distance, Bruno dancing with delight at every fresh yell extracted from Nero's terrified prisoner.

"That's all," the boy said at last.

"It *isn't* all!" cried Bruno. "There's three more in that pocket!"

Another hint from Sylvie to the Dog-King—another sharp yell from the thief, now convicted of lying also—and the remaining three apples were surrendered.

"Let him go, please," Sylvie said in Doggee, and the lad limped away at a great pace, stooping now and then to rub the ailing ankle, in fear, seemingly, that the 'crahmp' might attack it again.

Bruno ran back, with his booty, to the orchard wall, and pitched the apples over it one by one. "I's welly afraid *some* of them's gone under the wrong trees!" he panted, on overtaking us again.

"The *wrong* trees!" laughed Sylvie. "Trees *ca'n't* do wrong! There's no such things as *wrong* trees!"

"Then there's no such things as *right* trees, neither!" cried Bruno. And Sylvie gave up the point.

CHAPTER XVIII

HUSHABY BABY

"WAIT a minute, please!" she said to me. "I must make Nero *visible*, you know!"

"No, *please* don't!" cried Bruno, who had by this time mounted on the Royal back, and was twisting the Royal hair into a bridle. "It'll be *such* fun to have him like this!"

"Well, it *does* look funny," Sylvie admitted, and led the way to the farm-house, where the farmer's wife stood, evidently much perplexed at the weird procession now approaching her. "It's summat gone wrong wi' my spectacles, I doubt!" she murmured, as she took them off, and began diligently rubbing them with a corner of her apron.

Meanwhile Sylvie had hastily pulled Bruno down from his steed, and had just time to make His Majesty wholly visible before the spectacles were resumed.

All was natural, now; but the good woman still looked a little uneasy about it. "My eyesight's getting bad," she said, "but I see you *now*, my darlings! You'll give me a kiss, wo'n't you?"

Bruno got behind me, in a moment: however Sylvie put up *her* face, to be kissed, as representative of *both*, and we all went in together.

"Come to me, my little gentleman," said our hostess, lifting Bruno into her lap, "and tell me everything."

"I ca'n't," said Bruno. "There wouldn't be time. Besides, I don't *know* everything."

The good woman looked a little puzzled, and turned to Sylvie for help. "Does he like *riding?*" she asked.

"Yes, I *think* so," Sylvie gently replied. "He's just had a ride on *Nero*."

"Ah, Nero's a grand dog, isn't he? Were you ever outside a *horse*, my little man?"

"*Always!*" Bruno said with great decision. "Never was *inside* one. Was *oo?*"

Here I thought it well to interpose, and to mention the business on which we had come, and so relieved her, for a few minutes, from Bruno's perplexing questions.

"And those dear children will like a bit of cake, *I'll* warrant!" said the farmer's hospitable wife, when the business was concluded, as she opened her cupboard, and brought out a cake. "And don't you waste the crust, little gentleman!" she added, as she handed a good slice of it to Bruno. "You know what the poetry-book says about wilful waste?"

"No, I don't," said Bruno. "What doos he say about it?"

"Tell him, Bessie!" And the mother looked down, proudly and lovingly, on a rosy little maiden, who had just crept shyly into the room, and was leaning against her knee. "What's that your poetry-book says about wilful waste?"

"*For wilful waste makes woeful want,*" Bessie recited, in an almost inaudible whisper: "*and you may live to say 'How much I wish I had the crust that then I threw away!'*"

"Now try if *you* can say it, my dear! *For wilful——*"

"*For wifful*—sumfinoruvver—" Bruno began, readily enough; and then there came a dead pause. "Ca'n't remember no more!"

"Well, what do you *learn* from it, then? You can tell us *that*, at any rate?"

Bruno ate a little more cake, and considered: but the moral did not seem to him to be a very obvious one.

"Always to——" Sylvie prompted him in a whisper.

"Always to——" Bruno softly repeated: and then, with sudden inspiration, "always to look where it goes to!"

"Where *what* goes to, darling?"

"Why the *crust*, a course!" said Bruno. "Then, if I lived to say '*How much I wiss I had the crust—*' (and all that), I'd know where I frew it to!"

This new interpretation quite puzzled the good woman. She returned to the subject of 'Bessie.' "Wouldn't you like to see Bessie's doll, my dears! Bessie, take the little lady and gentleman to see Matilda Jane!"

"But we must be getting home," said I. "Would you call the little girls? Matilda Jane has seen enough of company, for *one* day, I'm sure!"

"I'll find 'em in a minute," said my hostess, as she rose to leave the room. "Maybe that young gentleman saw which way they went?"

"Where are they, Bruno?" I said.

"They ain't in the field," was Bruno's rather evasive reply, "'cause there's nothing but *pigs* there, and Sylvie isn't a pig. Now don't imperrupt me any more, 'cause I'm telling a story to this fly; and it won't attend!"

"They're among the apples, I'll warrant 'em!" said the Farmer's wife. So we left Bruno to finish his story, and went out into the orchard, where we soon came upon the children, walking sedately side by side, Sylvie carrying the doll, while little Bess carefully shaded its face, with a large cabbage-leaf for a parasol.

As soon as they caught sight of us, little Bess dropped her cabbage-leaf and came running to meet us, Sylvie following more slowly, as her precious charge evidently needed great care and attention.

"I'm it's Mamma, and Sylvie's the Head-Nurse," Bessie explained: "and Sylvie's taught me ever such a pretty song, for me to sing to Matilda Jane!"

"Let's hear it once more, Sylvie," I said, delighted at getting the chance I had long wished for, of hearing her sing. But Sylvie turned shy and frightened in a moment. "No, *please* not!" she said, in an earnest 'aside' to me. "Bessie knows it quite perfect now. Bessie can sing it!"

"Aye, aye! Let Bessie sing it!" said the proud mother. "Bessie has a bonny voice of her own," (this again was an 'aside' to me,) "though I say it as shouldn't!"

Bessie was only too happy to accept the 'encore.' So the plump little Mamma sat down at our feet, with her hideous daughter reclining stiffly across her lap (it was one of a kind that won't sit down, under *any* amount of persuasion), and, with a face simply beaming with delight, began the lullaby, in a shout that *ought* to have frightened the poor baby into fits.

The shout, with which she began, proved to

be only a momentary effort. After a very few notes, Bessie toned down, and sang on in a small but very sweet voice. At first her great black eyes were fixed on her mother, but soon

her gaze wandered upwards, among the apples, and she seemed to have quite forgotten that she had any other audience than her Baby, and her Head-Nurse, who once or twice supplied, almost inaudibly, the right note, when the singer was getting a little 'flat.'

"*Matilda Jane, you never look*
At any toy or picture-book:
I show you pretty things in vain—
You must be blind, Matilda Jane!

"*I ask you riddles, tell you tales,*
But all *our conversation fails:*
You never *answer me again—*
I fear you're dumb, Matilda Jane!

"*Matilda, darling, when I call,*
You never seem to hear at all:
I shout with all my might and main—
But you're so *deaf, Matilda Jane!*

"*Matilda Jane, you needn't mind:*
For, though you're deaf, and dumb, and blind,
There's some one *loves you, it is plain—*
And that is me, *Matilda Jane!*"

She sang three of the verses in a rather perfunctory style, but the last stanza evidently excited the little maiden. Her voice rose, ever clearer and louder: she had a rapt look on her face, as if suddenly inspired, and, as she sang the last few words, she clasped to her heart the inattentive Matilda Jane.

"Kiss it now!" prompted the Head-Nurse. And in a moment the simpering meaningless face of the Baby was covered with a shower of passionate kisses.

"What a bonny song!" cried the Farmer's wife. "Who made the words, dearie?"

"I—I think I'll look for Bruno," Sylvie said demurely, and left us hastily. The curious child seemed always afraid of being praised, or even noticed.

"Sylvie planned the words," Bessie informed us, proud of her superior information: "and Bruno planned the music—and *I* sang it!" (this last circumstance, by the way, we did not need to be told).

So we followed Sylvie, and all entered the parlour together. Bruno was still standing at the window, with his elbows on the sill. He had, apparently, finished the story that he was telling to the fly, and had found a new occupation. "Don't imperrupt!" he said as we came in. "I'm counting the Pigs in the field!"

"How many are there?" I enquired.

"About a thousand and four," said Bruno.

"You mean 'about a thousand,'" Sylvie corrected him. "There's no good saying '*and four*': you *ca'n't* be sure about the four!"

"And you're as wrong as ever!" Bruno exclaimed triumphantly. "It's just the *four* I *can* be sure about; 'cause they're here, grubbling under the window! It's the *thousand* I isn't pruffickly sure about!"

"But some of them have gone into the sty," Sylvie said, leaning over him to look out of the window.

"Yes," said Bruno; "but they went so slowly and so fewly, I didn't care to count *them*."

"We must be going, children," I said. "Wish Bessie good-bye." Sylvie flung her arms round the little maiden's neck, and kissed her: but Bruno stood aloof, looking unusually shy. ("I never kiss *nobody* but Sylvie!" he explained to me afterwards.) The farmer's wife showed us out: and we were soon on our way back to Elveston.

CHAPTER XIX

MEIN HERR

So I went on my lonely way, and, on reaching the Hall, I found the Earl standing at the garden-gate waiting for me.

"You will be at our farewell-party, this day fortnight," said the Earl. "Of course you will come. Muriel is anxious to gather all our friends around us once more, before we leave the place."

"Don't forget Tuesday week!" he said as we shook hands. "I only wish you could bring with you those charming children, that you introduced to us in the summer. Talk of the mystery of Mein Herr! That's *nothing* to the mystery that seems to attend *them!* I shall never forget those marvellous flowers!"

"I will bring them if I possibly can," I said. But how to *fulfil* such a promise, I mused to myself on my way back to my lodgings, was a problem entirely beyond my skill!

The days glided swiftly away and when, on our way to the drawing-room, I received from the housekeeper my little friends, clad in the daintiest of evening costumes, and looking, in the flush of expectant delight, more radiantly beautiful than I had ever seen them before, I felt no shock of surprise.

It would be best, I thought, to introduce them as soon as possible to some good-natured lady-guest, and I selected one. "I am sure you like children," I said. "May I introduce two little friends of mine? This is Sylvie—and this is Bruno."

The young lady kissed Sylvie very graciously. She would have done the same for *Bruno*, but he hastily drew back out of reach. "Their faces are new to me," she said.

"How far have you come, dear?"

Sylvie looked puzzled. "A mile or two, I *think*," she said doubtfully.

"A mile or *three*," said Bruno.

"You shouldn't say 'a mile or *three*,'" Sylvie corrected him.

The young lady nodded approval. "Sylvie's quite right. It isn't usual to say 'a mile or *three*.'"

"It would be usual—if we said it often enough," said Bruno.

It was the young lady's turn to look puzzled now. "He's very quick, for his age!" she murmured. "You're not more than seven, are you, dear?" she added aloud.

"I'm not so many as *that*," said Bruno. "I'm *one*. Sylvie's *one*. Sylvie and me is *two*. *Sylvie* taught me to count."

"Oh, I wasn't *counting* you, you know!" the young lady laughingly replied.

"Hasn't oo *learnt* to count?" said Bruno.

The young lady bit her lip. "Dear! What embarrassing questions he *does* ask!" she said in a half-audible 'aside.'

"Bruno, you shouldn't!" Sylvie said reprovingly.

"Shouldn't *what?*" said Bruno.

"You shouldn't ask—that sort of questions."

"*What* sort of questions?" Bruno mischievously persisted.

"What *she* told you not," Sylvie replied, with a shy glance at the young lady, and losing all sense of grammar in her confusion.

"Oo ca'n't pronounce it!" Bruno triumphantly cried. And he turned to the young lady, for sympathy in his victory. "I *knewed* she couldn't pronounce 'umbrella-sting'!"

The young lady thought it best to return to the arithmetical problem. "When I asked if you were *seven*, you know, I didn't mean 'how many *children?*' I meant 'how many *years*——'"

"Only got *two* ears," said Bruno. "Nobody's got *seven* ears."

"And you belong to this little girl?" the young lady continued, skilfully evading the anatomical problem.

"No, I doosn't belong to *her!*" said Bruno. "Sylvie belongs to *me!*" And he clasped his arms round her as he added "She are my very mine!"

"And, do you know," said the young lady,

"I've a little sister at home, exactly like *your* sister? I'm sure they'd love each other."

"They'd be very extremely useful to each other," Bruno said, thoughtfully. "And they wouldn't want no looking-glasses to brush their hair wiz."

"Why not, my child?"

"Why, each one would do for the other one's looking-glass, a-course!" cried Bruno.

By this time the room was getting crowded, as the guests, invited for the evening-party, were beginning to arrive, and Lady Muriel had to devote herself to the task of welcoming them, which she did with the sweetest grace imaginable. Sylvie and Bruno stood by her, deeply interested in the process.

"I hope you like my friends?" she said to them. "Specially my dear old friend, Mein Herr (What's become of him, I wonder? Oh, there he is!), that old gentleman in spectacles, with a long beard?"

"He's a grand old gentleman!" Sylvie said, gazing admiringly at 'Mein Herr,' who had settled down in a corner, from which his mild eyes beamed on us through a gigantic pair of spectacles. "And what a lovely beard!"

"What does he call his-self?" Bruno whispered.

"He calls himself 'Mein Herr,'" Sylvie whispered in reply.

Bruno shook his head impatiently. "That's what he calls his *hair*, not his *self*, oo silly!" He appealed to me. "What doos he call his *self*, Mister Sir?"

"That's the only name *I* know of," I said. "But he looks very lonely. Don't you pity his grey hairs?"

"I pities his *self*," said Bruno, still harping on the misnomer; "but I doosn't pity his *hair*, one bit. His *hair* ca'n't feel!"

"We met him this afternoon," said Sylvie. "We'd been to see Nero, and we'd had *such* fun with him, making him invisible again! And we saw that nice old gentleman as we came back."

"Well, let's go and talk to him, and cheer him up a little," I said: "and perhaps we shall find out what he calls himself."

The children came willingly. With one of

them on each side of me, I approached the corner occupied by 'Mein Herr.' "You don't object to *children*, I hope?" I began.

"*Crabbed age and youth cannot live together!*" the old man cheerfully replied, with a most genial smile. "Now take a good look at me, my children! You would guess me to be an *old* man, wouldn't you?"

"I don't know if oo're an *old* man," Bruno

answered, as the children, won over by the gentle voice, crept a little closer to him. "I thinks oo're *eighty-three*."

"He is very exact!" said Mein Herr.

"Is he anything like right?" I said.

"There are reasons," Mein Herr gently replied, "reasons which I am not at liberty to explain, for not mentioning *definitely* any Persons, Places, or Dates."

"Sylvie and me," said Bruno, "saw oo in the road, and oor hat were ever so high up! Weren't it, Sylvie?"

"There was a drop or two of rain falling," said Mein Herr, "so I put my hat on the top of my stick—as an umbrella, you know. As I came along the road," he continued, turning to me, "I was overtaken by——"

"——a shower of rain?" said Bruno.

"Well, it *looked* more like the tail of a dog," Mein Herr replied. "It was the most curious thing! Something rubbed affectionately against my knee. And I looked down. And I could see *nothing!* Only, about a yard off, there was a dog's tail, wagging all by itself!"

"Oh, *Sylvie!*" Bruno murmured reproachfully. "Oo didn't finish making him visible!"

"I'm *so* sorry!" Sylvie said, looking very penitent. "I meant to rub it along his back, but we were in such a hurry. We'll go and finish him to-morrow. Poor thing! Perhaps he'll get no supper to-night!"

"*Course* he won't!" said Bruno. "Nobody never gives bones to a dog's tail!"

Mein Herr looked from one to the other in blank astonishment. "I do not understand you," he said. "I had lost my way, and I was consulting a pocket-map, and somehow I had dropped one of my gloves, and this invisible *Something*, that had rubbed against my knee, actually brought it back to me!"

"Course he did!" said Bruno. "He's *welly* fond of fetching things."

Mein Herr looked so thoroughly bewildered that I thought it best to change the subject. "What a useful thing a pocket-map is!" I remarked.

CHAPTER XX

BRUNO'S PICNIC

THE silence that ensued was broken by the voice of the musical young lady, who had seated herself near us, and was conversing with one of the newly-arrived guests. "Well!" she said in a tone of scornful surprise. "We *are* to have something new in the way of music, it appears!"

I looked round for an explanation, and was nearly as much astonished as the speaker herself: it was *Sylvie* whom Lady Muriel was leading to the piano!

"Do try it, my darling!" she was saying. "I'm sure you can play very nicely!"

Sylvie looked round at me, with tears in her eyes. I tried to give her an encouraging smile, but it was evidently a great strain on the nerves of a child so wholly unused to be made an exhibition of, and she was frightened and unhappy.

But in a minute the hum had died away into absolute silence, and we all sat, entranced and breathless, to listen to such heavenly music that one held one's breath, fearful to lose a single note of it.

The Count hurried across the room in great excitement. "I *cannot* remember myself," he exclaimed, "of the name of this so charming an air! It is of an opera, most surely. Yet not even will the *opera* remind his name to me! What you call him, dear child?"

Sylvie looked round at him with a rapt expression of face. She had ceased playing, but her fingers still wandered fitfully over the keys. All fear and shyness had quite passed away now, and nothing remained but the pure joy of the music that had thrilled our hearts.

"The title of it!" the Count repeated impatiently. "How call you the opera?"

'I don't know what an opera *is*," Sylvie half-whispered.

"How, then, call you the *air?*"

"I don't know any name for it," Sylvie replied, as she rose from the instrument.

"But this is marvellous!" exclaimed the

Count, following the child, and addressing himself to me, as if I were the proprietor of this musical prodigy, and so *must* know the origin of her music. "You have heard her play this sooner—I would say 'before this occasion'? How call you the air?"

I shook my head; but was saved from more questions by Lady Muriel, who came up to petition the Count for a song.

The Count spread out his hands apologetically, and ducked his head. "But, Milady, I have already respected—I would say prospected—all your songs; and there shall be none fitted to my voice! They are not for basso voices!"

"Wo'n't you look at them again?" Lady Muriel implored.

"Let's help him!" Bruno whispered to Sylvie. "Let's get him—*you* know!"

Sylvie nodded. "Shall *we* look for a song for you?" she said sweetly to the Count.

"Mais *oui!*" the little man exclaimed.

"Of course we may!" said Bruno, while, each taking a hand of the delighted Count, they led him to the music-stand.

"There is still hope!" said Lady Muriel over her shoulder, as she followed them.

But at this moment Sylvie came to call Bruno, who had returned to my side, looking unusually serious. "*Do* come, Bruno!" she entreated. "You know we've nearly found it!"

But Bruno drew back. "The man called me names," he said with dignity.

"What names?" I enquired with some curiosity.

"I asked him," said Bruno, "which sort of song he liked. And he said '*A* song of *a* man, not of *a* lady.' And I said 'Shall Sylvie and me find you a song?' And he said 'Wait, eel!' And I'm *not* an eel, oo know!"

"I'm *sure* he didn't mean it!" Sylvie said earnestly. "It's something French—you know he ca'n't talk English so well as——"

Bruno relented visibly. "Course he knows no better, if he's Flench! Flenchmen *never* can speak English so goodly as *us!*" And Sylvie led him away, a willing captive.

"Nice children!" said the old man, taking off his spectacles and rubbing them carefully. Then he put them on again, and watched with an approving smile, while the children tossed over the heap of music, and we just caught Sylvie's reproving words, "We're *not* making hay, Bruno!"

"Now, I'll tell you a story."

"And I'll tell *oo* a story," said Bruno, beginning in a great hurry for fear of Sylvie getting the start of him: "once there were a Mouse—a little tiny Mouse—such a tiny little Mouse! Oo never saw such a tiny Mouse——"

"Did nothing ever happen to it, Bruno?" I asked. "Haven't you anything more to tell us, besides its being so tiny?"

"Nothing never happened to it," Bruno solemnly replied.

"Why did nothing never happen to it?" said Sylvie, who was sitting, with her head on Bruno's shoulder, patiently waiting for a chance of beginning *her* story.

"It were too tiny," Bruno explained.

"*That's* no reason!" I said. "However tiny it was, things might happen to it."

Bruno looked pityingly at me, as if he thought me very stupid. "It were too tiny," he repeated. "If anything happened to it, it would die—it were so *very* tiny!"

"Really that's enough about its being tiny!" Sylvie put in. "Haven't you invented any more about it?"

"Haven't invented no more yet."

"Well then, you shouldn't begin a story till you've invented more! Now be quiet, there's a good boy, and listen to *my* story."

And Bruno, having quite exhausted all his inventive faculty, by beginning in too great a hurry, quietly resigned himself to listening. "Tell about the other Bruno, please," he said coaxingly.

Sylvie put her arms round his neck, and began:—

"The wind was whispering among the trees," ("That wasn't good manners!" Bruno interrupted. "Never mind about manners," said Sylvie) "and it was evening—a nice moony evening, and the Owls were hooting——"

"Pretend they weren't Owls!" Bruno pleaded, stroking her cheek with his fat little hand. "I don't like Owls. Owls have such great big eyes. Pretend they were Chickens?"

"Are you afraid of their great big eyes, Bruno?" I said.

"Aren't '*fraid* of nothing," Bruno answered in as careless a tone as he could manage: "they're ugly with their great big eyes. I think if they cried, the tears would be as big—oh, as big as the moon!" And he laughed merrily. "Doos Owls cry ever, Mister Sir?"

"Owls cry never," I said gravely, trying to copy Bruno's way of speaking: "they've got nothing to be sorry for, you know."

"Oh, but they have!" Bruno exclaimed. "They're ever so sorry, 'cause they killed the poor little Mouses!"

"But they're not sorry when they're *hungry*, I suppose?"

"Oo don't know nothing about Owls!" Bruno scornfully remarked. "When they're hungry, they're very, *very* sorry they killed the little Mouses, 'cause if they *hadn't* killed them there'd be sumfin for supper, oo know!"

Bruno was evidently getting into a dangerously inventive state of mind, so Sylvie broke in with "Now I'm going on with the story. So the Owls—the Chickens, I mean—were looking to see if they could find a nice fat Mouse for their supper——"

"Pretend it was a nice 'abbit!" said Bruno.

"But it *wasn't* a nice habit, to kill Mouses," Sylvie argued. "I can't pretend *that!*"

"I didn't say '*habit*,' oo silly fellow!" Bruno

replied with a merry twinkle in his eye. "'*ab-bits*—that runs about in the fields!"

"Rabbit? Well it can be a Rabbit, if you like. But you mustn't alter my story so much, Bruno. A Chicken *couldn't* eat a Rabbit!"

"But it might have wished to see if it could try to eat it."

"Well, it wished to see if it could try—oh, really, Bruno, that's nonsense! I shall go back to the Owls."

"Well then, pretend they hadn't great eyes!"

"And they saw a little Boy," Sylvie went on, disdaining to make any further corrections. "And he asked them to tell him a story. And the Owls hooted and flew away——" ("Oo shouldn't say '*flewed*;' oo should say '*flied*,'" Bruno whispered. But Sylvie wouldn't hear.) "And he met a Lion. And he asked the Lion to tell him a story. And the Lion said 'yes,' it would. And, while the Lion was telling him the story, it nibbled some of his head off——"

"Don't say 'nibbled'!" Bruno entreated. "Only little things nibble—little thin sharp things, with edges——"

"Well then, it '*nubbled*,'" said Sylvie. "And

when it had nubbled *all* his head off, he went away, and he never said 'thank you'!"

"That were very rude," said Bruno. "If he couldn't speak, he might have nodded—no, he couldn't nod. Well, he might have shaked *hands* with the Lion!"

"Oh, I'd forgotten that part!" said Sylvie. "He *did* shake hands with it. He came back again, you know, and he thanked the Lion very much, for telling him the story."

"Then his head had growed up again?" said Bruno.

"Oh yes, it grew up in a minute. And the Lion begged pardon, and said it wouldn't nubble off little boys' heads—not never no more!"

Bruno looked much pleased at this change of events. "Now that are a *really* nice story!" he said. "*Aren't* it a nice story, Mister Sir?"

"Very," I said. "I would like to hear another story about that Boy."

"So would *I*," said Bruno, stroking Sylvie's cheek again. "*Please* tell about Bruno's Picnic; and don't talk about *nubbly* Lions!"

"I won't, if it frightens you," said Sylvie.

"*Flightens* me!" Bruno exclaimed indignantly. "It isn't *that!* It's 'cause 'nubbly' s such a grumbly word to say—when one person's got her head on another person's shoulder. When she talks like that," he explained to me, "the talking goes down bofe sides of my face—all the way to my chin—and it *doos* tickle so! It's enough to make a beard grow, that it is!"

He said this with great severity, but it was evidently meant for a joke: so Sylvie laughed—a delicious musical little laugh, and laid her soft cheek on the top of her brother's curly head, as if it were a pillow, while she went on with the story. "So this Boy——"

"But it wasn't *me*, oo know!" Bruno interrupted. "And oo needn't try to look as if it was, Mister Sir!"

I represented, respectfully, that I was trying to look as if it wasn't.

"—he was a middling good Boy——"

"He were a *welly* good Boy!" Bruno corrected her. "And he never did nothing he wasn't told to do——"

"*That* doesn't make a good Boy!" Sylvie said contemptuously.

"That *do* make a good Boy!" Bruno insisted.

Sylvie gave up the point. "Well, he was a *very* good Boy, and he always kept his promises, and he had a big cupboard——"

"—for to keep all his promises in!" cried Bruno.

"If he kept *all* his promises," Sylvie said, with a mischievous look in her eyes, "he wasn't like *some* Boys I know of!"

"He had to put *salt* with them, a-course," Bruno said gravely: "oo ca'n't keep promises when there isn't any salt. And he kept his birthday on the second shelf."

"How long did he keep his birthday?" I asked. "I never can keep *mine* more than twenty-four hours."

"Why, a birthday *stays* that long by itself!" cried Bruno. "Oo doosn't know how to keep birthdays! This Boy kept *his* a whole year!"

"And then the next birthday would begin," said Sylvie. "So it would be his birthday *always*."

"So it were," said Bruno. "Doos *oo* have treats on *oor* birthday, Mister Sir?"

"Sometimes," I said.

"When oo're *good*, I suppose?"

"Why, it *is* a sort of treat, being good, isn't it?" I said.

"A sort of *treat!*" Bruno repeated. "It's a sort of *punishment*, *I* think!"

"Oh, Bruno!" Sylvie interrupted, almost sadly. "How *can* you?"

"Well, but it *is*," Bruno persisted. "Why, look here, Mister Sir! *This* is being good!" And he sat bolt upright, and put on an absurdly solemn face. "First oo must sit up as straight as pokers——"

"—as *a* poker," Sylvie corrected him.

"—as straight as *pokers*," Bruno firmly repeated. "Then oo must clasp oor hands—*so*. Then—'Why hasn't oo brushed oor hair? Go and brush it *toreckly!*' Then—'Oh, Bruno, oo mustn't dog's-ear the daisies!' Did oo learn *oor* spelling wiz daisies, Mister Sir?"

"I want to hear about that Boy's *Birthday*," I said.

Bruno returned to the story instantly. "Well, so this Boy said 'Now it's my Birthday!' And so—I'm tired!" he suddenly broke off, laying his head on Sylvie's lap. "Sylvie knows it best. Sylvie's grown-upper than me. Go on, Sylvie!"

Sylvie patiently took up the thread of the story again. "So he said 'Now it's my Birthday. Whatever shall I do to keep my Birthday? All *good* little Boys——" (Sylvie turned away from Bruno, and made a great pretence of whispering to *me*) "—all *good* little Boys— Boys that learn their lessons quite perfect— they always keep their birthdays, you know. So of course *this* little Boy kept *his* Birthday."

"Oo may call him Bruno, if oo like," the little fellow carelessly remarked. "It weren't *me*, but it makes it more interesting."

"So Bruno said to himself 'The properest thing to do is to have a Picnic, all by myself, on the top of the hill. And I'll take some Milk, and some Bread, and some Apples: and first and foremost, I want some *Milk!*' So, first and foremost, Bruno took a milk-pail——"

"And he went and milkted the Cow!" Bruno put in.

"Yes," said Sylvie, meekly accepting the new verb. "And the Cow said 'Moo! What are you going to do with all that Milk?' And Bruno said 'Please'm, I want it for my Picnic.' And the Cow said 'Moo! But I hope you wo'n't *boil* any of it?' And Bruno said 'No, *indeed* I wo'n't! New Milk's so nice and so warm, it wants no boiling!'"

"It doesn't want no boiling," Bruno offered as an amended version.

"So Bruno put the Milk in a bottle. And then Bruno said 'Now I want some Bread!' So he went to the Oven, and he took out a delicious new Loaf. And the Oven——"

"—ever so light and so puffy!" Bruno impatiently corrected her. "Oo shouldn't leave out so many words!"

Sylvie humbly apologised. "—a delicious new Loaf, ever so light and so puffy. And the Oven said——" Here Sylvie made a long pause. "Really I don't know *what* an Oven begins with, when it wants to speak!"

Both children looked appealingly at me; but I could only say, helplessly, "I haven't the least idea! *I* never heard an Oven speak!"

For a minute or two we all sat silent; and then Bruno said, very softly, "Oven begins wiz 'O'."

"*Good* little boy!" Sylvie exclaimed. "He does his spelling *very* nicely. *He's cleverer than he knows!*" she added, aside, to *me*. "So the Oven said 'O! What are you going to do with all that Bread?' And Bruno said 'Please——' Is an Oven 'Sir' or ''m,' would you say?" She looked to me for a reply.

"*Both*, I think," seemed to me the safest thing to say.

Sylvie adopted the suggestion instantly. "So Bruno said 'Please, Sirm, I want it for my Picnic.' And the Oven said 'O! But I hope you wo'n't *toast* any of it?' And Bruno said 'No, *indeed* I wo'n't! New Bread's so light and so puffy, it wants no toasting!'"

"It never doesn't want no toasting," said Bruno. "I *wiss* oo wouldn't say it so short!"

"So Bruno put the Bread in the hamper. Then Bruno said 'Now I want some Apples!' So he took the hamper, and he went to the

Apple-Tree, and he picked some lovely ripe Apples. And the Apple-Tree said "—— Here followed another long pause.

Bruno adopted his favourite expedient of tapping his forehead; while Sylvie gazed earnestly upwards, as if she hoped for some suggestion from the birds, who were singing merrily among the branches overhead. But no result followed.

"What *does* an Apple-tree begin with, when it wants to speak?" Sylvie murmured despairingly, to the irresponsive birds.

At last, taking a leaf out of Bruno's book, I ventured on a remark. "Doesn't 'Apple-tree' always begin with 'Eh!'?"

"Why, of *course* it does! How *clever* of you!" Sylvie cried delightedly.

Bruno jumped up, and patted me on the head. I tried not to feel conceited.

"So the Apple-Tree said 'Eh! What are you going to do with all those Apples?' And Bruno said 'Please, Sir, I want them for my Picnic.' And the Apple-Tree said 'Eh! But I hope you wo'n't *bake* any of them? And Bruno said 'No, *indeed* I wo'n't! Ripe

Apples are so nice and so sweet, they want no baking!'"

"They never doesn't——" Bruno was beginning, but Sylvie corrected herself before he could get the words out.

"'They never doesn't nohow want no baking.' So Bruno put the Apples in the hamper, along with the Bread, and the bottle of Milk. And he set off to have a Picnic, on the top of the hill, all by himself——"

"He wasn't greedy, oo know, to have it all by himself," Bruno said, patting me on the cheek to call my attention; "'cause he hadn't got no brothers and sisters."

"It was very sad to have no *sisters*, wasn't it?" I said.

"Well, I don't know," Bruno said thoughtfully; "'cause he hadn't no lessons to do. So he didn't mind."

Sylvie went on. "So, as he was walking along the road, he heard behind him such a curious sort of noise—a sort of a Thump! Thump! Thump! 'Whatever *is* that?' said Bruno. 'Oh, I know!' said Bruno. 'Why, it's only my Watch a-ticking!'"

"*Were* it his Watch a-ticking?" Bruno asked me, with eyes that fairly sparkled with mischievous delight.

"No doubt of it!" I replied. And Bruno laughed exultingly.

"Then Bruno thought a little harder. And he said 'No! It *ca'n't* be my Watch a-ticking; because I haven't *got* a Watch!'"

Bruno peered up anxiously into my face, to see how I took it. I hung my head, and put a thumb into my mouth, to the evident delight of the little fellow.

"So Bruno went a little further along the road. And then he heard it again, that queer noise—Thump! Thump! Thump! 'What ever *is* that?' said Bruno. 'Oh, I know!' said Bruno. 'Why, it's only the Carpenter a-mending my Wheelbarrow!'"

"*Were* it the Carterpenter a-mending his Wheelbarrow?" Bruno asked me.

I brightened up, and said "It *must* have been!" in a tone of absolute conviction.

Bruno threw his arms round Sylvie's neck. "Sylvie!" he said, in a perfectly audible whisper. "He says it *must* have been!"

"Then Bruno thought a little harder. And he said 'No! It *ca'n't* be the Carpenter a-mending my Wheelbarrow, because I haven't *got* a Wheelbarrow!'"

This time I hid my face in my hands, quite unable to meet Bruno's look of triumph.

"So Bruno went a little further along the road. And then he heard that queer noise again—Thump! Thump! Thump! So he thought he'd look round, *this* time, just to *see* what it was. And what should it be but a great Lion!"

"A great big Lion," Bruno corrected her.

"A great big Lion. And Bruno was ever so frightened, and he ran——"

"No, he wasn't *flightened* a bit!" Bruno interrupted. (He was evidently anxious for the reputation of his namesake.) "He runned away to get a good look at the Lion; 'cause he wanted to see if it were the same Lion what used to nubble little Boys' heads off; and he wanted to know how big it was!"

"Well, he ran away, to get a good look at the Lion. And the Lion trotted slowly after him. And the Lion called after him, in a very gentle voice, 'Little Boy, little Boy! You needn't be afraid of *me!* I'm a very *gentle* old Lion now. I *never* nubble little Boys' heads off, as I used to do.' And so Bruno said 'Don't you *really*, Sir? Then what do you live on?' And the Lion——"

"Oo *see* he weren't a bit flightened!" Bruno said to me, patting my cheek again, "'cause he remembered to call it 'Sir,' oo know."

I said that no doubt that was the *real* test whether a person was frightened or not.

"And the Lion said 'Oh, I live on bread-and-butter, and cherries, and marmalade, and plum-cake——'"

"—and *apples!*" Bruno put in.

"Yes, 'and apples.' And Bruno said 'Wo'n't you come with me to my Picnic?' And the Lion said 'Oh, I should like it *very much indeed!*' And Bruno and the Lion went away together." Sylvie stopped suddenly.

"Is that *all?*" I asked, despondingly.

"Not *quite* all," Sylvie slily replied. "There's a sentence or two more. Isn't there, Bruno?"

"Yes," with a carelessness that was evidently put on: "just a sentence or two more."

"And, as they were walking along, they looked over a hedge, and who should they see but a little black Lamb! And the Lamb was ever so frightened. And it ran——"

"It were *really* flightened!" Bruno put in.

"It ran away. And Bruno ran after it. And he called 'Little Lamb! You needn't be afraid of *this* Lion! It *never* kills things! It lives on cherries, and marmalade——'"

"— and *apples!*" said Bruno. "Oo *always* forgets the apples!"

"And Bruno said 'Wo'n't you come with us to my Picnic?' And the Lamb said 'Oh, I should like it *very much indeed*, if my Ma will let me!' And Bruno said 'Let's go and ask your Ma!' And they went to the old Sheep. And Bruno said 'Please, may your little Lamb come to my Picnic?' And the Sheep said 'Yes, if it's learnt all its lessons.' And the Lamb said 'Oh yes, Ma! I've learnt *all* my lessons!'"

"Pretend it hadn't any lessons!" Bruno earnestly pleaded.

"Oh, that would never do!" said Sylvie. "I ca'n't leave out all about the lessons! And the old Sheep said 'Do you know your A B C yet? Have you learnt A?' And the Lamb said 'Oh yes, Ma! I went to the A-field, and I helped them to make A!' 'Very good, my child! And have you learnt B?' 'Oh yes, Ma! I went to the B-hive, and the B gave me some honey!' 'Very good, my child! And have you learnt C?' 'Oh yes, Ma! I went to the C-side, and I saw the ships sailing on the C!' 'Very good, my child! You may go to Bruno's Picnic.'

"So they set off. And Bruno walked in the middle, so that the Lamb mightn't see the Lion——"

"It were *flightened*," Bruno explained.

"Yes, and it trembled so; and it got paler and paler; and, before they'd got to the top of the hill, it was a *white* little Lamb—as white as snow!"

"But *Bruno* weren't flightened!" said the owner of that name. "So *he* staid black!"

"No, he *didn't* stay black! He staid *pink!*"

laughed Sylvie. "I shouldn't kiss you like this, you know, if you were *black!*"

"Oo'd *have* to!" Bruno said with great decision. "Besides, Bruno wasn't *Bruno*, oo know—I mean, Bruno wasn't *me*—I mean—don't talk nonsense, Sylvie!"

"I wo'n't do it again!" Sylvie said very

humbly. "And so, as they went along, the Lion said 'Oh, I'll tell you what I used to do when I was a young Lion. I used to hide behind trees, to watch for little Boys.'" (Bruno cuddled a little closer to her.) "'And, if a little thin scraggy Boy came by, why, I used to let him go. But, if a little fat juicy——'"

Bruno could bear no more. "Pretend he wasn't juicy!" he pleaded, half-sobbing.

"Nonsense, Bruno!" Sylvie briskly replied. "It'll be done in a moment! '——if a little fat juicy Boy came by, why, I used to spring out and gobble him up! Oh, you've no *idea* what a delicious thing it is—a little juicy Boy!' And Bruno said 'Oh, if you please, Sir, *don't* talk about eating little boys! It makes me so *shivery!*'"

The real Bruno shivered, in sympathy with the hero.

"And the Lion said 'Oh, well, we wo'n't talk about it, then! I'll tell you what happened on my wedding day——'"

"I like *this* part better," said Bruno, patting my cheek to keep me awake.

"'There was, oh, such a lovely wedding-breakfast! At *one* end of the table there was a large plum-pudding. And at the other end there was a nice roasted *Lamb!* Oh, you've no *idea* what a delicious thing it is—a nice roasted Lamb!' And the Lamb said 'Oh, if you please, Sir, *don't* talk about eating Lambs! It makes me so *shivery!*' And the Lion said 'Oh, well, we wo'n't talk about it, then!'"

"So, when they got to the top of the hill, Bruno opened the hamper: and he took out the Bread, and the Apples, and the Milk: and they ate, and they drank. And when they'd finished the Milk, and eaten half the Bread and half the Apples, the Lamb said 'Oh, my paws is so sticky! I want to wash my paws!' And the Lion said 'Well, go down the hill, and wash them in the brook, yonder. We'll wait for you!'"

"It never comed back!" Bruno solemnly whispered to me.

But Sylvie overheard him. "You're not to whisper, Bruno! It spoils the story! And when the Lamb had been gone a long time, the Lion said to Bruno 'Do go and see after that silly little Lamb! It must have lost its way.' And Bruno went down the hill. And when he got to the brook, he saw the Lamb sitting on the bank: and who should be sitting by it but an old Fox!"

"Don't know who *should* be sitting by it," Bruno said thoughtfully to himself. "A old Fox *were* sitting by it."

"And the old Fox were saying," Sylvie went on, for once conceding the grammatical point, "'Yes, my dear, you'll be ever so happy with us, if you'll only come and see us! I've got three little Foxes there, and we do love little Lambs so dearly!' And the Lamb said 'But you never *eat* them, do you, Sir?' And the Fox said 'Oh, no! What, *eat* a Lamb? We never *dream* of doing such a thing!' So the Lamb said 'Then I'll come with you.' And off they went, hand in hand."

"That Fox were welly extremely wicked, *weren't* it?" said Bruno.

"No, no!" said Sylvie, rather shocked at such violent language. "It wasn't quite so bad as that!"

"Well, I mean, it wasn't nice," the little fellow corrected himself.

"And so Bruno went back to the Lion. 'Oh, come quick!' he said. 'The Fox has taken the Lamb to his house with him! I'm *sure* he means to eat it!' And the Lion said 'I'll come as quick as ever I can!' And they trotted down the hill."

"Do oo think he caught the Fox, Mister Sir?" said Bruno. I shook my head, not liking to speak: and Sylvie went on.

"And when they got to the house, Bruno looked in at the window. And there he saw the three little Foxes sitting round the table, with their clean pinafores on, and spoons in their hands——"

"Spoons in their hands!" Bruno repeated in an ecstasy of delight.

"And the Fox had got a great big knife—all ready to kill the poor little Lamb——" ("Oo needn't be flightened, Mister Sir!" Bruno put in, in a hasty whisper.)

"And just as he was going to do it, Bruno heard a great ROAR——" (The real Bruno put his hand into mine, and held tight), "and the Lion came *bang* through the door, and the next moment it had bitten

off the old Fox's head! And Bruno jumped in at the window, and went leaping round the room, and crying out 'Hooray! Hooray! The old Fox is dead! The old Fox is dead!'"

Bruno got up in some excitement. "May I do it now?" he enquired.

Sylvie was quite decided on this point. "Wait till afterwards," she said. "The speeches come next, don't you know? You always love the speeches, *don't* you?"

"Yes, I doos," said Bruno: and sat down again.

"The Lion's speech. 'Now, you silly little Lamb, go home to your mother, and never listen to old Foxes again. And be very good and obedient.'

"The Lamb's speech. 'Oh, indeed, Sir, I will, Sir!' and the Lamb went away." ("But *oo* needn't go away!" Bruno explained. "It's quite the nicest part—what's coming now!" Sylvie smiled. She liked having an appreciative audience.)

"The Lion's speech to Bruno. 'Now, Bruno, take those little Foxes home with you, and teach them to be good obedient little Foxes! Not like that wicked old thing there, that's got no head!'" ("That hasn't got no head," Bruno repeated.)

"Bruno's speech to the Lion. 'Oh, indeed, Sir, I will, Sir!' And the Lion went away." ("It gets betterer and betterer, now," Bruno whispered to me, "right away to the end!")

"Bruno's speech to the little Foxes. 'Now, little Foxes, you're going to have your first lesson in being good. I'm going to put you into the hamper, along with the Apples and the Bread: and you're not to eat the Apples: and you're not to eat the Bread: and you're not to eat *anything*—till we get to my house: and then you'll have your supper.'

"The little Foxes' speech to Bruno. The little Foxes said nothing.

CHAPTER XXI

LITTLE FOXES

"So Bruno put the Apples into the hamper —and the little Foxes—and the Bread—" ("They had picnicked all the Milk," Bruno explained in a whisper) "—and he set off to go to his house." ("We're getting near the end now," said Bruno.)

"And, when he had got a little way, he thought he would look into the hamper, and see how the little Foxes were getting on."

"So he opened the door——" said Bruno.

"Oh, Bruno!" Sylvie exclaimed, "*you're* not telling the story! So he opened the door, and behold, there were no Apples! So Bruno said 'Eldest little Fox, have *you* been eating the

Apples?' And the eldest little Fox said 'No no no!'" (It is impossible to give the tone in which Sylvie repeated this rapid little 'No no no!' The nearest I can come to it is to say that it was much as if a young and excited duck had tried to quack the words. It was too quick for a quack, and yet too harsh to be anything else.) "Then he said 'Second little Fox, have *you* been eating the Apples?' And the second little Fox said 'No no no!' Then he said 'Youngest little Fox, have *you* been eating the Apples?' And the youngest little Fox *tried* to say 'No no no!' but its mouth was so full, it couldn't, and it only said 'Wauch! Wauch! Wauch!' And Bruno looked into its mouth. And its mouth was full of Apples! And Bruno shook his head, and he said 'Oh dear, oh dear! What bad creatures these Foxes are!'"

Bruno was listening intently: and, when Sylvie paused to take breath, he could only just gasp out the words "About the Bread?"

"Yes," said Sylvie, "the Bread comes next. So he shut the door again; and he went a little further; and then he thought he'd just peep in once more. And behold, there was no Bread!" ("What do 'behold' *mean?*" said Bruno. "Hush!" said Sylvie.) "And he said 'Eldest little Fox, have *you* been eating the Bread?' And the eldest little Fox said 'No no no!' 'Second little Fox, have *you* been eating the Bread?' And the second little Fox only said 'Wauch! Wauch! Wauch!' And Bruno looked into its mouth, and its mouth was full of Bread!" ("It might have chokeded it," said Bruno.) "So he said 'Oh dear, oh dear! What *shall* I do with these Foxes?' And he went a little further." ("Now comes the most interesting part," Bruno whispered.)

"And when Bruno opened the hamper again, what do you think he saw?" ("Only *two* Foxes!" Bruno cried in a great hurry.) "You shouldn't tell it so quick. However, he *did* see only *two* Foxes. And he said 'Eldest little Fox, have you been eating the youngest little Fox?' And the eldest little Fox said 'No no no!' 'Second little Fox, have *you* been eating the youngest little Fox?' And the second little Fox did its very best to say 'No no no!' but it could only say 'Weuchk!

Weuchk! Weuchk!' And when Bruno looked into its mouth, it was half full of Bread, and half full of Fox!" (Bruno said nothing in the pause this time. He was beginning to pant a little, as he knew the crisis was coming.)

"And when he'd got nearly home, he looked once more into the hamper, and he saw——"

"Only——" Bruno began, but a generous thought struck him, and he looked at me. "*Oo* may say it, *this* time, Mister Sir!" he whispered. It was a noble offer, but I wouldn't rob him of the treat. "Go on, Bruno," I said, "you say it much the best." "Only—but—*one*—Fox!" Bruno said with great solemnity.

"'Eldest little Fox,'" Sylvie said, dropping the narrative-form in her eagerness, "'you've been *so* good that I can hardly believe *you've* been disobedient: but I'm *afraid* you've been eating your little sister?' And the eldest little Fox said 'Whihuauch! Whihuauch!' and then it choked. And Bruno looked into its mouth, and it *was* full!" (Sylvie paused to take breath, and Bruno lay back among the daisies, and looked at me triumphantly. "Isn't it *grand*, Mister Sir?" said he. I tried hard to assume a critical tone. "It's grand," I said: "but it frightens one so!" "Oo may sit a little closer to *me*, if oo like," said Bruno.)

"And so Bruno went home: and took the hamper into the kitchen, and opened it. And he saw——" Sylvie looked at *me*, this time, as if she thought I had been rather neglected and ought to be allowed *one* guess, at any rate.

"He ca'n't guess!" Bruno cried eagerly. "I 'fraid I *must* tell him! There weren't—*nuffin* in the hamper!" I shivered in terror, and Bruno clapped his hands with delight. "He *is* flightened, Sylvie! Tell the rest!"

"So Bruno said 'Eldest little Fox have you been eating *yourself*, you wicked little Fox?' And the eldest little Fox said 'Whihuauch!' And then Bruno saw there was only its *mouth* in the hamper! So he took the mouth, and he opened it, and shook, and shook! And at last he shook the little Fox out of its own mouth! And then he said, 'Open your mouth again, you wicked little thing!' And he shook, and shook! And he shook out the second little Fox! And he said 'Now open *your* mouth!' And he shook, and shook! And he shook out the youngest little Fox, and all the Apples, and all the Bread!

"And then Bruno stood the little Foxes up against the wall: and he made them a little speech. 'Now, little Foxes, you've begun very wickedly—and you'll have to be punished. First you'll go up to the nursery, and wash your faces, and put on clean pinafores. Then you'll hear the bell ring for supper. Then you'll come down : and *you wo'n't have any supper:* but you'll have a good *whipping!* Then you'll go to bed. Then in the morning you'll hear the bell ring for breakfast. *But you wo'n't have any breakfast!* You'll have a good *whipping!* Then you'll have your lessons. And, perhaps, if you're *very* good, when dinner-time comes, you'll have a little dinner, and no more whipping!'" ("How *very* kind he was!" I whispered to Bruno. "*Middling* kind," Bruno corrected me gravely.)

"So the little Foxes ran up to the nursery. And soon Bruno went into the hall, and rang the big bell. 'Tingle, tingle, tingle! Supper, supper, supper!' Down came the little Foxes, in such a hurry for their supper! Clean pinafores! Spoons in their hands! And, when they got into the dining-room, there was ever such a white table-cloth on the table! But there was nothing on it but a big whip. And they had *such* a whipping!" (I put my handkerchief to my eyes, and Bruno hastily climbed upon my knee and stroked my face. "Only *one* more whipping, Mister Sir!" he whispered. "Don't cry more than oo ca'n't help!")

"And the next morning early, Bruno rang the big bell again. 'Tingle, tingle, tingle! Breakfast, breakfast, breakfast!' Down came the little Foxes! Clean pinafores! Spoons in their hands! No breakfast! Only the big whip! Then came lessons," Sylvie hurried on, for I still had my handkerchief to my eyes. "And the little Foxes were ever so good! And they learned their lessons backwards, and forwards, and upside-down. And at last Bruno rang the big bell again. 'Tingle, tingle, tingle! Dinner, dinner, dinner!' And when the little Foxes came down——" ("Had they clean pinafores on?" Bruno enquired. "Of course!" said Sylvie. "And spoons?" "Why, you *know* they had!" "Couldn't be *certain*," said Bruno.) "——they came as slow as slow! And they said 'Oh! There'll be no dinner! There'll only be the big whip!' But, when they got into the room, they saw the most *lovely* dinner!" ("Buns?" cried Bruno, clapping his hands.) "Buns, and cake, and——" ("——and jam?" said Bruno.) "Yes, jam—

and soup—and——" ("——and *sugar plums!*" Bruno put in once more; and Sylvie seemed satisfied.)

"And ever after that, they *were* such good little Foxes! They did their lessons as good as gold—and they never did what Bruno told them not to—and they never ate each other any more—and *they never ate themselves!*"

The story came to an end so suddenly, it almost took my breath away; however, I did my best to make a pretty speech of thanks. "I'm sure it's very—very—very much so, I'm sure!" I seemed to hear myself say.

CHAPTER XXII

SYLVIE'S MUSIC

AND, in the silence that followed, the stanzas of the song "Tottles" rang through the room.

The conclusion of the song was followed by quite a chorus of thanks and compliments from all parts of the room, which the gratified singer responded to by bowing low in all directions. "It is to me a great privilege," he said to Lady Muriel, "to have met with this so marvellous a song. The accompaniment to him is so strange, so mysterious: it is as if a new music were to be invented! I will play him once again so as that to show you what I mean." He returned to the piano, but the song had vanished.

The bewildered singer searched through the heap of music lying on an adjoining table, but it was not there, either. Lady Muriel helped in the search: others soon joined: the excitement grew. "What *can* have become of it?" exclaimed Lady Muriel. Nobody knew: one thing only was certain, that no one had been near the piano since the Count had sung the last verse of the song.

"Nevare mind him!" he said, most good-naturedly. "I shall give it you with memory alone!" He sat down, and began vaguely fingering the notes; but nothing resembling the tune came out. Then he, too, grew excited. "But what oddness! How much of singularity! That I might lose, not the words alone, but the tune also—that is quite curious, I suppose?"

We all supposed it, heartily.

"It was that sweet little boy, who found it for me," the Count suggested. "Quite perhaps *he* is the thief?"

"Of course he is!" cried Lady Muriel. "Bruno! Where are you, my darling?"

But no Bruno replied: it seemed that the

two children had vanished as suddenly, and as mysteriously, as the song.

"They are playing us a trick!" Lady Muriel gaily exclaimed. "This is only an *ex tempore* game of Hide-and-Seek! That little Bruno is an embodied Mischief!"

The suggestion was a welcome one to most of us, for some of the guests were beginning to look decidedly uneasy. A general search was set on foot with much enthusiasm: curtains were thrown back and shaken, cupboards opened, and ottomans turned over; but the number of possible hiding-places proved to be strictly limited; and the search came to an end almost as soon as it had begun.

"They must have run out while we were wrapped up in the song," Lady Muriel said, addressing herself to the Count, who seemed more agitated than the others; "and no doubt they've found their way back to the housekeeper's room."

"Not by *this* door!" was the earnest protest of a knot of two or three gentlemen, who had been grouped round the door (one of them actually leaning against it) for the last half-hour, as they declared. "*This* door has not been opened since the song began!"

An uncomfortable silence followed this announcement.

Not yet at the end of her resources, Lady Muriel rang the bell. "Ask the housekeeper to step here," she said, "and to bring the children's walking things with her."

"I've brought them, my lady," said the obsequious housekeeper, entering after another minute of silence. "I thought the young lady would have come to my room to put on her boots. Here's your boots, my love!" she added cheerfully, looking in all directions for the children. There was no answer, and she turned to Lady Muriel with a puzzled smile. "Have the little darlings hid themselves?"

"I don't see them, just now," Lady Muriel replied, rather evasively. "You can leave their things here, Wilson. *I'll* dress them, when they're ready to go."

Finally, the things were piled together on the centre-ottoman, and the guests, despairing of seeing the children again, began to wish good-night and leave the house.

There were only some eight or nine left—to whom the Count was explaining, for the twentieth time, how he had had his eye on the children during the last verse of the song; how he had then glanced round the room, to see what effect "de great chest-note" had had upon his audience; and how, when he looked back again, they had both disappeared—when exclamations of dismay began to be heard on all sides, the Count hastily bringing his story to an end to join in the outcry.

The walking-things had all disappeared!

After the utter failure of the search for the *children*, there was a very half-hearted search made for their *apparel.* The remaining guests seemed only too glad to get away, leaving only the Count and our four selves.

The Count sank into an easy-chair, and panted a little.

"Who then *are* these dear children, I pray you?" he said. "Why come they, why go they, in this so little ordinary a fashion? That the music should make itself to vanish—that the hats, the boots, should make themselves to vanish—how is it, I pray you?"

"I've no idea where they are!" was all I could say, on finding myself appealed to, by general consent, for an explanation.

The Count seemed about to ask further questions, but checked himself.

"The hour makes himself to become late," he said. "I wish to you a very good night, my Lady. I betake myself to my bed—to dream—if that indeed I be not dreaming now!" And he hastily left the room.

"I'm *so* glad I've seen Sylvie!" said Lady Muriel the next morning. "My heart went out to the child the first moment that I saw her—— Listen!" she broke off suddenly. "That's Sylvie singing! I'm sure of it! Don't you know her voice?"

"I have heard *Bruno* sing, more than once," I said: "but I never heard Sylvie."

"I have only heard her *once*," said Lady Muriel. "It was that day when you brought us those mysterious flowers. The children had run out into the garden: and Sylvie was singing, under the trees, a song I had never heard before. The words were something like 'I think it is Love, I feel it is Love.'

Listen!" she cried, breaking off again in her excitement. "That *is* her voice, and that's the very song!"

The song ceased just as they came into sight: but, to my delight, Bruno instantly said "Let's sing it all again, Sylvie! It *did* sound so pretty!" And Sylvie replied "Very well. It's *you* to begin, you know."

So Bruno began, in the sweet childish treble I knew so well:—

"*Say, what is the spell, when her fledgelings are cheeping,*
That lures the bird home to her nest?
Or wakes the tired mother, whose infant is weeping,
To cuddle and croon it to rest?
What's the magic that charms the glad babe in her arms,
Till it cooes with the voice of the dove?"

Sylvie's part was a very short one—only a few words—and she sang it timidly, and very low indeed, scarcely audibly, but the *sweetness* of her voice was simply indescribable.

"*'Tis a secret, and so let us whisper it low—*
And the name of the secret is Love!"

The figures of the children became vague and shadowy, like glimmering meteors: while their voices rang together in exquisite harmony as they sang:—

"*For I think it is Love,*
For I feel it is Love,
For I'm sure it is nothing but Love!"

Bruno again sang by himself:—

"*Say, whence is the voice that, when anger is burning,*
Bids the whirl of the tempest to cease?
That stirs the vexed soul with an aching—a yearning
For the brotherly hand-grip of peace?
Whence the music that fills all our being—that thrills
Around us, beneath, and above?"

Sylvie sang more courageously this time: the words seemed to carry her away, out of herself:—

"*'Tis a secret: none knows how it comes, how it goes:*
But the name of the secret is Love!"

And clear and strong the chorus rang out :—

> "*For I think it is Love,*
> *For I feel it is Love,*
> *For I'm sure it is nothing but Love!*"

Once more we heard Bruno's delicate little voice alone :—

> "*Say whose is the skill that paints valley and hill.*
> *Like a picture so fair to the sight?*
> *That flecks the green meadow with sunshine and shadow,*
> *Till the little lambs leap with delight?*"

And again uprose that silvery voice, whose angelic sweetness I could hardly bear :—

> "*'Tis a secret untold to hearts cruel and cold,*
> *Though 'tis sung, by the angels above,*
> *In notes that ring clear for the ears that can hear—*
> *And the name of the secret is Love!*"

And then Bruno joined in again with

> "*For I think it is Love,*
> *For I feel it is Love,*
> *For I'm sure it is nothing but Love!*"

"That *are* pretty!" the little fellow exclaimed, as the children passed us.

"No use to try and stop them!" I said, as they passed away into the shadows. "Why, they could not even *see* us!"

"No use at all," Lady Muriel echoed with a sigh. "One would *like* to meet them again, in living form! But I feel, somehow, *that* can never be. They have passed out of *our* lives!"

CHAPTER XXIII

QUESTIONS AND ANSWERS

THE lonely evening seemed long and tedious: yet I lingered on, watching the dying fire, and there I saw now the Professor's jolly round face, beaming with delight. "You're welcome, my little ones!" he seemed to say.

"I told them you were coming. Your rooms are all ready for you. And the Emperor and the Empress—well, I think they're rather pleased than otherwise! In fact, Her Highness said 'I hope they'll be in time for the Banquet!' Those were her very words, I assure you!"

"Will Uggug be at the Banquet?" Bruno

asked. And both children looked uneasy at the dismal suggestion.

"Why, of course he will!" chuckled the Professor. "Why, it's his *birthday*, don't you know? And his health will be drunk, and all that sort of thing. What would the Banquet be without *him?*"

"Ever so much nicer," said Bruno. But he said it in a *very* low voice, and nobody but Sylvie heard him.

The Professor chuckled again. "It'll be a jolly Banquet, now *you've* come, my little man! I *am* so glad to see you again!"

"I 'fraid we've been very long in coming," Bruno politely remarked.

"Well, yes," the Professor assented. "However, you're very short now you're come: that's *some* comfort." And he went on to enumerate the plans for the day. "The Lecture comes first," he said. "*That* the Empress *insists* on. She says people will eat so much at the Banquet, they'll be too sleepy to attend to the Lecture afterwards—and perhaps she's right. There'll just be a little *refreshment*, when the people first arrive. *Then* comes the Lecture——"

"What? The Lecture you were getting ready—ever so long ago?" Sylvie enquired.

"Yes—that's the one," the Professor rather reluctantly admitted. "It *has* taken a goodish time to prepare. I've got so many other things to attend to. For instance, I'm Court-Physician. I have to keep all the Royal Servants in good health—and that reminds me!" he cried, ringing the bell in a great hurry. "This is Medicine-Day! We only give Medicine once a week. If we were to begin giving it every day, the bottles would *soon* be empty!"

"But if they were ill on the *other* days?" Sylvie suggested.

"What, ill on the wrong *day!*" exclaimed the Professor. "Oh, that would never do! A servant would be dismissed *at once*, who was ill on the wrong day! This is the Medicine for *today*," he went on, taking down a large jug from a shelf. "I mixed it, myself, first thing this morning. Taste it!" he said, holding out the jug to Bruno. "Dip in your finger, and taste it!"

Bruno did so, and made such an excruciatingly wry face that Sylvie exclaimed, in alarm, "Oh, Bruno, you mustn't!"

"It's welly extremely nasty!" Bruno said, as his face resumed its natural shape.

"Nasty?" said the Professor. "Why, of *course* it is! What would Medicine be, if it wasn't *nasty?*"

"Nice," said Bruno.

"I was going to say—" the Professor faltered rather taken aback by the promptness of Bruno's reply, "——that *that* would never do! Medicine *has* to be nasty, you know. Be good enough to take this jug down into the Servants' Hall," he said to the footman who answered the bell: "and tell them it's their Medicine for *today*."

"Which of them is to drink it?" the footman asked, as he carried off the jug.

"Oh, I've not settled *that* yet!" the Professor briskly replied. "I'll come and settle that, soon. Tell them not to begin, on any account, till I come! It's really *wonderful*," he said, turning to the children, "the success I've had in curing Diseases! Here are some of my memoranda." He took down from the shelf a heap of little bits of paper, pinned together in twos and threes. "Just look at *this* set, now. '*Under-Cook Number Thirteen recovered from Common Fever—Febris Communis.*' And now see what's pinned to it. '*Gave Under-Cook Number Thirteen a Double Dose of Medicine.*' *That's* something to be proud of, *isn't* it?"

"But which happened *first?*" said Sylvie, looking very much puzzled.

The Professor examined the papers carefully. "They are not *dated*, I find," he said with a slightly dejected air: "so I fear I ca'n't tell you. But they *both* happened: there's no doubt of *that*. The *Medicine's* the great thing, you know. The *Diseases* are much less important. You can keep a *Medicine* for years and years: but nobody ever wants to keep a *Disease!* By the way, come and look at the platform. The Gardener asked me to come and see if it would do. We may as well go before it gets dark."

"We'd like to, very much!" Sylvie replied. "Come, Bruno, put on your hat. Don't keep the dear Professor waiting!"

"Ca'n't find my hat!" the little fellow sadly replied. "I were rolling it about. And it's rolled itself away!"

"Maybe it's rolled in *there*," Sylvie suggested, pointing to a dark recess, the door of which stood half open: and Bruno ran in to look. After a minute he came slowly out again, looking very grave, and carefully shut the cupboard-door after him.

"It aren't in there," he said, with such unusual solemnity, that Sylvie's curiosity was roused.

"What *is* in there, Bruno?"

"There's cobwebs—and two spiders—" Bruno thoughtfully replied, checking off the catalogue on his fingers, "——and the cover of a picture-book—and a tortoise—and a dish of nuts—and an old man."

"An old man!" cried the Professor, trotting across the room in great excitement. "Why, it must be the Other Professor, that's been lost for ever so long!"

He opened the door of the cupboard wide: and there he was, the Other Professor, sitting in a chair, with a book on his knee, and in the act of helping himself to a nut from a dish, which he had taken down off a shelf just within his reach. He looked round at us, but

said nothing till he had cracked and eaten the nut. Then he asked the old question. "Is the Lecture all ready?"

"It'll begin in an hour," the Professor said,

evading the question. "First, comes the Banquet——"

"The Banquet!" cried the Other Professor, springing up, and filling the room with a cloud of dust. Then I'd better go and—and brush myself a little. What a state I'm in!"

"He *does* want brushing!" the Professor said, with a critical air, "Here's your hat, little man! I had put it on by mistake. I'd quite forgotten I had *one* on, already. Let's go and look at the platform."

"And there's that nice old Gardener singing still!" Bruno exclaimed in delight, as we went out into the garden. "I do believe he's been singing that very song ever since we went away!"

"Why, of course he has!" replied the Professor. "It wouldn't be the thing to leave off, you know."

"Wouldn't be *what* thing?" said Bruno: but the Professor thought it best not to hear the question. "What are you doing with that hedgehog?" he shouted at the Gardener, whom they found standing upon one foot, singing softly to himself, and rolling a hedgehog up and down with the other foot.

"Well, I wanted fur to know what hedgehogs lives on: so I be a-keeping this here hedgehog—fur to see if it eats potatoes——"

"Much better keep a potato," said the Professor; "and see if hedgehogs eat it!"

"That be the roight way, sure-ly!" the delighted Gardener exclaimed. "Be you come to see the platform?"

"Aye, aye!" the Professor cheerily replied, "And the children have come back, you see!"

The Gardener looked round at them with a grin. Then he led the way to the Pavilion; and as he went he sang:—

"*He looked again, and found it was*
A Double Rule of Three:
'*And all its Mystery,' he said,*
'*Is clear as day to me!*'"

"You've been *months* over that song," said the Professor. "Isn't it finished yet?"

"There be only one verse more," the Gardener sadly replied. And, with tears streaming down his cheeks, he sang the last verse :—

> "*He thought he saw an Argument*
> *That proved he was the Pope:*
> *He looked again, and found it was*
> *A Bar of Mottled Soap.*
> '*A fact so dread,' he faintly said,*
> '*Extinguishes all hope!*' "

Choking with sobs, the Gardener hastily stepped on a few yards ahead of the party, to conceal his emotion.

"Did *he* see the Bar of Mottled Soap?" Sylvie enquired, as we followed.

"Oh, certainly!" said the Professor. "That song is his own history, you know."

Tears of an ever-ready sympathy glittered in Bruno's eyes. "I's *welly* sorry he isn't the Pope!" he said. "Aren't *you* sorry, Sylvie?"

"Well—I hardly know," Sylvie replied in the vaguest manner. "Would it make him any happier?" she asked the Professor.

"It wouldn't make the *Pope* any happier," said the Professor. "Isn't the platform *lovely?*" he asked, as we entered the Pavilion.

"I've put an extra beam under it!" said the Gardener, patting it affectionately as he spoke. "And now it's that strong, as—as a mad elephant might dance upon it!"

"Thank you *very* much!" the Professor heartily rejoined. "I don't know that we shall exactly require—but it's convenient to know." And he led the children upon the platform, to explain the arrangements to them. "Here are three seats, you see, for the Emperor and the Empress and Prince Uggug. But there must be two more chairs here!" he said, looking down at the Gardener. "One for Lady Sylvie, and one for the smaller animal!"

"And may I help in the Lecture?" said Bruno. "I can do some conjuring-tricks."

"Well, it's not exactly a *conjuring* lecture," the Professor said, as he arranged some curious-looking machines on the table. "However, what can you do? Did you ever go through a table, for instance?"

"Often!" said Bruno. "*Haven't* I, Sylvie?"

The Professor was evidently surprised, though he tried not to show it. "This must be looked into," he muttered to himself, taking out a note-book. "And first—what kind of table?"

"Tell him!" Bruno whispered to Sylvie, putting his arms round her neck.

"Tell him yourself," said Sylvie.

"Ca'n't," said Bruno. "It's a *bony* word."

"Nonsense!" laughed Sylvie. "You can say it well enough, if you only try. Come!"

"Muddle——" said Bruno. "That's a bit of it."

"*What* does he say?" cried the bewildered Professor.

"He means the multiplication-table," Sylvie explained.

The Professor looked annoyed, and shut up his note-book again. "Oh, that's *quite* another thing," he said.

"It are ever so many other things," said Bruno. "*Aren't* it, Sylvie?"

A loud blast of trumpets interrupted this conversation. "Why, the entertainment has *begun!*" the Professor exclaimed, as he hurried the children into the Reception-Saloon. "I had no idea it was so late!"

A small table, containing cake and wine,

stood in a corner of the Saloon; and here we found the Emperor and Empress waiting for us.

"So you're come at last!" the Emperor sulkily remarked, as the Professor and the children took their places.

There was a rather awkward pause: the Professor evidently didn't know how to begin. The Empress leant forwards, and whispered to him. "A few jokes, you know, Professor—just to put people at their ease!"

"True, true, Madam!" the Professor meekly replied. "This little boy——"

"*Please* don't make any jokes about *me!*" Bruno exclaimed, his eyes filling with tears.

"I wo'n't if you'd rather I didn't," said the kind-hearted Professor. "It was only something about a Ship's Buoy: a harmless pun—but it doesn't matter." Here he turned to the crowd and addressed them in a loud voice. "Learn your A's!" he shouted. "Your B's! Your C's! And your D's! *Then* you'll be at your ease!"

There was a roar of laughter from all the assembly, and then a great deal of confused whispering. "*What* was it he said? Something about bees, I fancy——"

"It's difficult to get things started," the Professor remarked to Bruno. "When once we get started, it'll go on all right, you'll see."

"If oo want to startle people," said Bruno, "oo should put live frogs on their backs."

But Sylvie put her hand over his mouth, and said, "He's rather tired, I think. He wants the Lecture to begin."

"I want the *supper* to begin," Bruno corrected her.

CHAPTER XXIV

THE LECTURE

But now the Professor was in the act of beginning the long-expected Lecture.

"In Science—in fact, in most things—it is usually best *to begin at the beginning*. In *some* things, of course, it's better to begin at the *other* end. For instance, if you wanted to paint a dog green, it *might* be best to begin with the *tail*, as it doesn't bite at *that* end. And so——"

"May *I* help oo?" Bruno interrupted.

"Help me to do *what?*" said the puzzled Professor, looking up for a moment, but keeping his finger on the book he was reading from, so as not to lose his place.

"To paint a dog green!" cried Bruno. "*Oo* can begin wiz its *mouf*, and I'll—— "

"No, no!" said the Professor. "We haven't got to the *Experiments* yet. And so," returning to his note-book, "I'll give you the Axioms of Science. After that I shall exhibit some Specimens. Then I shall explain a Process or two. And I shall conclude with a few Experiments. An *Axiom*, you know, is a thing that you accept without contradiction. For instance, if I were to say 'Here we are!', that would be accepted without any contradiction, and it's a nice sort of remark to *begin* a conversation with. So it would be an *Axiom*. Or again, supposing I were to say 'Here we are not!', *that* would be—— "

"——a fib!" cried Bruno.

"Oh, *Bruno!*" said Sylvie in a warning whisper. "Of course it would be an *Axiom*, if the Professor said it!"

"——that would be accepted, if people were civil," continued the Professor; "so it would be *another* Axiom."

"It *might* be an Axledum," Bruno said: "but it wouldn't be *true!*"

"The *First* Axiom," the Professor read out in a great hurry, "consists of these words, '*Whatever is, is.*' And the Second consists of *these* words, '*Whatever isn't, isn't.*' We will now go on to the *Specimens.* The first tray contains Crystals and other Things." He drew it towards him, and again referred to his note-book. "Some of the labels—owing to insufficient adhesion——" Here he stopped again, and carefully examined the page with his eyeglass. "I can't quite read the rest of the sentence," he said at last, "but it *means* that the labels have come loose, and the Things have got mixed——"

"Let *me* stick 'em on again!" cried Bruno eagerly, and began licking them like postage-stamps, and dabbing them down upon the Crystals and the other Things. But the Professor hastily moved the tray out of his reach. "They *might* get fixed to the *wrong* Specimens, you know!" he said.

"Oo shouldn't have any *wrong* peppermints in the tray!" Bruno boldly replied. "*Should* he, Sylvie?"

But Sylvie only shook her head.

"Our first Specimen," he went on, carefully opening a small jar, "is——" here he removed the lid, and a large beetle instantly darted out, and with an angry buzz went straight out of the Pavilion, "——is—or rather, I should say," looking sadly into the empty jar, "it *was*—a curious kind of Blue Beetle. Did any one happen to remark—as it went past—three blue spots under each wing?"

Nobody had remarked them.

"Ah, well!" the Professor said with a sigh. "It's a pity. Unless you remark that kind of thing *at the moment*, it's very apt to get overlooked! The *next* Specimen, at any rate, will not fly away! It is—in short, or perhaps, more correctly, at *length*—an *Elephant*. You will observe——" Here he beckoned to the Gardener to come up on the platform, and with his help began putting together what looked like an enormous dog-kennel, with short tubes projecting out of it on both sides.

"But we've seen *Elephants* before," the Emperor grumbled.

"Yes, but not through a *Megaloscope!*" the Professor eagerly replied. "You know you ca'n't see a *Flea*, properly, without a *magnifying*-glass—what we call a *Microscope*. Well, just in the same way, you ca'n't see an *Elephant*, properly, without a *minimifying*-glass. There's one in each of these little tubes. And *this* is a *Megaloscope!* The Gardener will now bring in the next Specimen. Please open *both* curtains, down at the end there, and make way for the Elephant!"

There was a general rush to the sides of the Pavilion, and all eyes were turned to the open end, watching for the return of the Gardener, who had gone away singing "*He thought he saw an Elephant That practised on a Fife!*" There was silence for a minute: and then his harsh voice was heard again in the distance. "*He looked again*—come up, then! *He looked again, and found it was*—woa back! *and found it was A letter from his*—make way there! He's a-coming!"

And in marched, or waddled—it is hard to say which is the right word—an Elephant, on its hind-legs, and playing on an enormous fife which it held with its fore-feet.

The Professor hastily threw open a large

door at the end of the Megaloscope, and the huge animal, at a signal from the Gardener, dropped the fife, and obediently trotted into

the machine, the door of which was at once shut by the Professor. "The Specimen is now ready for observation!" he proclaimed. "It is exactly the size of the Common Mouse —*Mus Communis!*"

There was a general rush to the tubes, and the spectators watched with delight the minikin creature, as it playfully coiled its trunk round the Professor's extended finger, finally taking its stand upon the palm of his hand, while he carefully lifted it out, and carried it off to exhibit to the Imperial party.

"Isn't it a *darling?*" cried Bruno. "May I stroke it, please? I'll touch it *welly* gently!"

"The next Specimen," the Professor proclaimed, after carefully placing the little Elephant in the tray, among the Crystals and other Things, "is a *Flea*, which we will enlarge for the purposes of observation." Taking a small pill-box from the tray, he advanced to the Megaloscope, and reversed all the tubes. "The Specimen is ready!" he cried, with his eye at one of the tubes, while he carefully emptied the pill-box through a little hole at the side. "It is now the size of the Common Horse—*Equus Communis!*"

There was another general rush, to look through the tubes, and the Pavilion rang with shouts of delight, through which the Professor's anxious tones could scarcely be heard. "Keep the door of the Microscope *shut!*" he cried. "If the creature were to escape, *this size*, it would——" But the mischief was done. The door had swung open, and in another moment the Monster had got out, and was trampling down the terrified, shrieking spectators.

But the Professor's presence of mind did not desert him. "Undraw those curtains!" he shouted. It was done. The monster gathered its legs together, and in one tremendous bound vanished into the sky.

"Where *is* it?" said the Emperor, rubbing his eyes.

"In the next Province, I fancy," the Professor replied. "That jump would take it at *least* five miles! The next thing is to explain a Process or two. But I find there is hardly room enough to operate—the smaller animal is rather in my way——"

'Who does he mean?" Bruno whispered to Sylvie.

"He means *you!*" Sylvie whispered back. "Hush!"

"Be kind enough to move—angularly—to *this* corner," the Professor said, addressing himself to Bruno.

Bruno hastily moved his chair in the direction indicated. "Did I move angrily enough?" he enquired. But the Professor was once more absorbed in his Lecture, which he was reading from his note-book.

"I will now explain the Process of—the name is blotted, I'm sorry to say. It will be illustrated by a number of—of——" here he examined the page for some time, and at last said "It seems to be either 'Experiments' or 'Specimens'——"

"Let it be *Experiments*," said the Emperor. "We've seen plenty of *Specimens*."

"Certainly, certainly!" the Professor assented. "We will have some Experiments."

"May *I* do them?" Bruno eagerly asked.

"Oh dear no!" The Professor looked dismayed. "I really don't know what would happen if *you* did them!"

"Nor nobody doosn't know what'll happen if *oo* doos them!" Bruno retorted.

"Our First Experiment requires a Machine. I divide my subject," he went on, "into three parts——"

"I think I'll get down!" Bruno whispered to Sylvie. "It aren't nice to be divided!"

"He hasn't got a knife, silly boy!" Sylvie whispered in reply. "Stand still! You'll break all the bottles!"

"The first part is to take hold of the knobs," putting them into Bruno's hands. "The second part is——" Here he turned the handle, and, with a loud "Oh!", Bruno dropped both the knobs, and began rubbing his elbows.

The Professor chuckled in delight. "It had a sensible effect. *Hadn't* it?" he enquired.

"No, it hadn't a *sensible* effect!" Bruno said indignantly. "It were very silly indeed. It jingled my elbows, and it banged my back, and it crinkled my hair, and it buzzed among my bones!"

"I'm sure it *didn't!*" said Sylvie. "You're only inventing!"

"Oo doosn't know nuffin about it!" Bruno replied. "Oo wasn't there to see. Nobody ca'n't go among my bones. There isn't room!"

"Our Second Experiment," the Professor announced, as Bruno returned to his place, still thoughtfully rubbing his elbows, "is the production of that seldom-seen-but-greatly-to-be-admired phenomenon, Black Light!—would any one like to get under the blankets and see it?"

Dead silence followed this appeal: but at last Bruno said "*I'll* get under, if it won't jingle my elbows."

Satisfied on this point, Bruno crawled under the blankets, and, after a minute or two, crawled out again, very hot and dusty, and with his hair in the wildest confusion.

"What did you see?" Sylvie eagerly enquired.

"I saw *nuffin!*" Bruno sadly replied. "It were too dark!"

"He has described the appearance of the thing exactly!" the Professor exclaimed with enthusiasm. "Black Light, and Nothing, look so extremely alike, at first sight, that I don't wonder he failed to distinguish them! Shall I repeat the Experiment?"

"No, no! Don't trouble yourself!" was the general cry. And we all trooped off, in hot haste, to the Banqueting-Hall, where the feast had already begun.

CHAPTER XXV

THE BANQUET

No time was lost in helping the dishes, and very speedily every guest found his plate filled with good things.

"I have always maintained the principle," the Professor began, "that it is a good rule to take some food—occasionally. The great advantage of dinner-parties——" he broke off suddenly. "Why, actually here's the Other Professor!" he cried. "And there's no place left for him!"

The Other Professor came in reading a large book, which he held close to his eyes. One result of his not looking where he was going was that he tripped up, as he crossed the

Saloon, flew up into the air, and fell heavily on his face in the middle of the table.

"*What* a pity!" cried the kind-hearted Professor, as he helped him up.

"It wouldn't be *me*, if I didn't trip," said the Other Professor.

The Professor looked much shocked. "Almost *anything* would be better than *that!*" he exclaimed. "It never does," he added, aside to Bruno, "to be anybody else, does it?"

To which Bruno gravely replied "I's got nuffin on my plate."

The Professor hastily put on his spectacles, to make sure that the *facts* were all right, to begin with: then he turned his jolly round face upon the unfortunate owner of the empty plate. "And what would you like next, my little man?"

"Well," Bruno said, a little doubtfully, "I think I'll take some plum-pudding, please—while I think of it."

"Oh, Bruno!" (This was a whisper from Sylvie.) "It isn't good manners to ask for a dish before it comes!"

And Bruno whispered back "But I might forget to ask for some, when it comes, oo know

—I *do* forget things, sometimes," he added, seeing Sylvie about to whisper more.

And *this* assertion Sylvie did not venture to contradict.

Meanwhile a chair had been placed for the Other Professor, between the Empress and Sylvie. Sylvie found him a rather uninteresting neighbour: in fact, she couldn't afterwards remember that he had made more than *one* remark to her during the whole banquet, and that was "What a comfort a Dictionary is!" (She told Bruno, afterwards, that she had been too much afraid of him to say more than "Yes, Sir," in reply; and that had been the end of their conversation. On which Bruno expressed a very decided opinion that *that* wasn't worth calling a "conversation" at all. "Oo should have asked him a riddle!" he added triumphantly. "Why, *I* asked the Professor *three* riddles! One was that one you asked me in the morning, 'How many pennies is there in two shillings?' And another was——" "Oh, Bruno!" Sylvie interrupted. "*That* wasn't a riddle!" "It *were!*" Bruno fiercely replied.)

By this time a waiter had supplied Bruno

with a plateful of *something*, which drove the plum-pudding out of his head.

"Another advantage of dinner-parties," the Professor cheerfully explained, for the benefit of any one that would listen, "is that it helps you to *see* your friends. If you want to *see* a man, offer him something to eat. It's the same rule with a mouse."

"This Cat's very kind to the Mouses," Bruno said, stooping to stroke a remarkably fat specimen of the race, that had just waddled into the room, and was rubbing itself affectionately against the leg of his chair. "Please, Sylvie, pour some milk in your saucer. Pussie's ever so thirsty!"

"Why do you want *my* saucer?" said Sylvie. "You've got one yourself!"

"Yes, I know," said Bruno: "but I wanted *mine* for to give it some *more* milk in."

Sylvie looked unconvinced; however, it seemed quite impossible for her *ever* to refuse what her brother asked; so she quietly filled her saucer with milk, and handed it to Bruno, who got down off his chair to administer it to the cat.

"Has the cat had enough?" Sylvie asked.

This was to Bruno, who had brought back the saucer only half-emptied.

But Bruno did not hear the question. "There's somebody scratching at the door and wanting to come in," he said. And he scrambled down off his chair, and went and cautiously peeped out through the door-way.

"Who was it wanted to come in?" Sylvie asked, as he returned to his place.

"It were a Mouse," said Bruno. "And it peepted in. And it saw the Cat. And it said 'I'll come in another day.' And I said 'Oo needn't be flightened. The Cat's *welly* kind to Mouses.' And it said 'But I's got some imporkant business, what I *must* attend to.' And it said 'I'll call again to-morrow.' And it said 'Give my love to the Cat.'"

"What a fat cat it is!" said the Professor. "It's quite a wonder!"

"It was awfully fat when it camed in," said Bruno: "so it would be more wonderfuller if it got thin all in a minute."

"And that was the reason, I suppose," the Professor suggested, "why you didn't give it the rest of the milk?"

"No," said Bruno. "It were a betterer reason. I tooked the saucer up 'cause it were so discontented!"

"It doesn't look so to *me*," said the Professor. "What made you think it was discontented?"

"'Cause it grumbled in its throat."

"Oh, Brūno!" cried Sylvie. "Why, that's the way cats show they're *pleased!*"

Bruno looked doubtful. "It's not a good way," he objected. "Oo wouldn't say *I* were pleased if I made that noise in my throat!"

"What a singular boy!" the Professor whispered to himself: but Bruno had caught the words.

"What do it mean to say 'a *singular* boy ?"' he whispered to Sylvie.

"It means *one* boy," Sylvie whispered in return. "And *plural* means two or three."

"Then I's welly glad I *is* a singular boy!" Bruno said with great emphasis. "It would be *horrid* to be two or three boys! P'raps they wouldn't play with me!"

"Why *should* they?" said the Other Professor, suddenly waking up out of a deep reverie. "They might be asleep, you know."

"Couldn't, if *I* was awake," Bruno said cunningly.

"Oh, but they might indeed!" the Other Professor protested. "Boys don't all go to sleep at once, you know. So these boys—but who are you talking about?"

"He *never* remembers to ask that first!" the Professor whispered to the children.

"Why, the rest of *me*, a-course!" Bruno exclaimed triumphantly. "Supposing I was two or three boys!"

The Other Professor sighed, and seemed to be sinking back into his reverie; but suddenly brightened up again, and addressed the Professor. "There's nothing more to be done *now*, is there?"

"Well, there's the dinner to finish," the Professor said with a bewildered smile: "and the heat to bear. I hope you'll enjoy the dinner—such as it is; and that you won't mind the heat—such as it isn't."

The sentence *sounded* well, but somehow I couldn't quite understand it; and the Other Professor seemed to be no better off. "Such as it isn't *what?*" he peevishly enquired.

"It isn't as hot as it might be," the Professor replied, catching at the first idea that came to hand.

"Ah, I see what you mean *now!*" the Other Professor graciously remarked. "It's very badly expressed, but I quite see it *now!* Thirteen minutes and a half ago," he went on, looking first at Bruno and then at his watch as he spoke, "you said 'this Cat's very kind to the Mouses.' It must be a singular animal!"

"So it *are*," said Bruno after carefully examining the Cat, to make sure how many there were of it.

"But how do you know it's kind to the Mouses—or, more correctly speaking, the *Mice?*"

"'Cause it *plays* with the Mouses," said Bruno; "for to amuse them, oo know."

"But that is just what I *don't* know," the Other Professor rejoined. "My belief is, it plays with them to *kill* them!"

"Oh, that's quite a *accident!*" Bruno began, so eagerly, that it was evident he had already propounded this very difficulty to the Cat. "It 'splained all that to me, while it were drinking the milk. It said 'I teaches the Mouses new games: the Mouse likes it ever so much.' It said 'Sometimes little accidents happens: sometimes the Mouses kills theirselves.' It said 'I's always *welly* sorry, when the Mouses kills theirselves.' It said——"

"If it was so *very* sorry," Sylvie said, rather disdainfully, "it wouldn't *eat* the Mouses after they'd killed themselves!"

"It said," answered Bruno, 'Dead Mouses *never* objecks to be eaten.' It said 'There's no use wasting good Mouses.' It said 'Wifful ——' sumfinoruvver. It said 'And oo may live to say "How much I wiss I had the Mouse that then I frew away!"' It said——"

"It hadn't *time* to say such a lot of things!" Sylvie interrupted indignantly.

"Oo doosn't know how Cats speaks!" Bruno rejoined contemptuously. "Cats speaks *welly* quick!"

CHAPTER XXVI

THE PIG-TALE

By this time the appetites of the guests seemed to be nearly satisfied, and even *Bruno* had the resolution to say, when the Professor offered him a fourth slice of plum-pudding, "I thinks three helpings is enough!"

Suddenly the Professor started as if he had been electrified. "Why, I had nearly forgotten the most important part of the entertainment! The Other Professor is to recite a Tale of a Pig—I mean a Pig-Tale," he corrected himself. "It has Introductory Verses at the beginning, and at the end."

"It ca'n't have Introductory Verses at the *end*, can it?" said Sylvie.

"Wait till you hear it," said the Professor: "then you'll see. I'm not sure it hasn't some in the *middle*, as well." Here he rose to his feet, and there was an instant silence through the Banqueting-Hall: they evidently expected a speech.

"Ladies, and gentlemen," the Professor began, "the Other Professor is so kind as to recite a Poem. The title of it is 'The Pig-Tale.' He never recited it before!" (General cheering among the guests.) "He will never recite it again!" (Frantic excitement, and wild cheering all down the hall, the Professor himself mounting the table in hot haste, to lead the cheering, and waving his spectacles in one hand and a spoon in the other.)

Then the Other Professor got up, and began:—

Little Birds are dining
Warily and well
Hid in mossy cell:
Hid, I say, by waiters
Gorgeous in their gaiters—
I've a Tale to tell.

Little Birds are feeding
Justices with jam,
Rich in frizzled ham:
Rich, I say, in oysters
Haunting shady cloisters—
That is what I am.

Little Birds are teaching
Tigresses to smile,
Innocent of guile:
Smile, I say, not smirkle—
Mouth a semicircle,
That's the proper style!

Little Birds are sleeping
All among the pins,
Where the loser wins:
Where, I say, he sneezes
When and how he pleases—
So the Tale begins.

There was a Pig that sat alone
Beside a ruined Pump:
By day and night he made his moan—
It would have stirred a heart of stone
To see him wring his hoofs and groan,
Because he could not jump.

A certain Camel heard him shout—
A Camel with a hump.
"*Oh, is it Grief, or is it Gout?*
What is this bellowing about?"
That Pig replied, with quivering snout,
"*Because I cannot jump!*"

That Camel scanned him, dreamy-eyed.
"*Methinks you are too plump.*
I never knew a Pig so wide—
That wobbled so from side to side—
Who could, however much he tried,
Do such a thing as jump!

"*Yet mark those trees, two miles away,*
All clustered in a clump:
If you could trot there twice a day,
Nor ever pause for rest or play,
In the far future—Who can say?—
You may be fit to jump."

That Camel passed, and left him there
Beside the ruined Pump.
Oh, horrid was that Pig's despair!
His shrieks of anguish filled the air.
He wrung his hoofs, he rent his hair.
Because he could not jump.

There was a Frog that wandered by—
A sleek and shining lump:
Inspected him with fishy eye,

And said "O Pig, what makes you cry?"
And bitter was that Pig's reply,
"Because I cannot jump!"

That Frog he grinned a grin of glee,
And hit his chest a thump.
"O Pig," he said, "be ruled by me,
And you shall see what you shall see.
This minute, for a trifling fee,
I'll teach you how to jump!

"You may be faint from many a fall,
And bruised by many a bump:
But, if you persevere through all,
And practise first on something small,
Concluding with a ten-foot wall,
You'll find that you can *jump!"*

That Pig looked up with joyful start:
"Oh Frog, you are *a trump!*
Your words have healed my inward smart—
Come, name your fee and do your part:
Bring comfort to a broken heart,
By teaching me to jump!"

"My fee shall be a mutton-chop,
My goal this ruined Pump.
Observe with what an airy flop

I plant myself upon the top!
Now bend your knees and take a hop,
For that's the way to jump!"

Uprose that Pig, and rushed, full whack,
Against the ruined pump:
Rolled over like an empty sack,
And settled down upon his back,
While all his bones at once went 'Crack!'
It was a fatal jump.

When the Other Professor had recited this Verse, he went across to the fire-place, and put his head up the chimney. In doing this, he lost his balance, and fell head-first into the empty grate, and got so firmly fixed there that it was some time before he could be dragged out again.

Bruno had had time to say "I thought he wanted to see how many peoples was up the chimbley."

And Sylvie had said "*Chimney*—not chimbley."

And Bruno had said "Don't talk 'ubbish!"

All this while the Other Professor was being extracted.

"You must have blacked your face!" the Empress said anxiously. "Let me send for some soap?"

"Thanks, no," said the Other Professor, keeping his face turned away. "Black's quite a respectable colour. Besides, soap would be no use without water."

Keeping his back well turned away from the audience, he went on with the Introductory Verses:—

Little Birds are writing
Interesting books,
To be read by cooks:
Read, I say, not roasted—
Letterpress, when toasted,
Loses its good looks.

Little Birds are playing
Bagpipes on the shore,
Where the tourists snore:
"Thanks!" they cry. "'Tis thrilling!
Take, oh take this shilling!
Let us have no more!"

Little Birds are bathing
Crocodiles in cream,
Like a happy dream:
Like, but not so lasting—
Crocodiles, when fasting,
Are not all they seem!

That Camel passed, as Day grew dim
Around the ruined Pump.
"O broken heart! O broken limb!
It needs," that Camel said to him,
"Something more fairy-like and slim,
To execute a jump!"

That Pig lay still as any stone,
And could not stir a stump:
Nor ever, if the truth were known,

Was he again observed to moan,
Nor ever wring his hoofs and groan,
Because he could not jump.

That Frog made no remark, for he
Was dismal as a dump:
He knew the consequence must be
That he would never get his fee—
And still he sits, in miserie,
Upon that ruined Pump!

"It's a miserable story!" said Bruno. "It begins miserably, and it ends miserablier. I think I shall cry. Sylvie, please lend me your handkerchief."

"I haven't got it with me," Sylvie whispered.

"Then I wo'n't cry," said Bruno manfully.

"There are more Introductory Verses to come," said the Other Professor, "but I'm hungry." He sat down, cut a large slice of cake, put it on Bruno's plate, and gazed at his own empty plate in astonishment.

"Where did you get that cake?" Sylvie whispered to Bruno.

"He gived it me," said Bruno.

"But you shouldn't ask for things! You *know* you shouldn't!"

"I *didn't* ask," said Bruno, taking a fresh mouthful: "he *gived* it me."

Sylvie considered this for a moment: then she saw her way out of it. "Well, then, ask him to give *me* some!"

"You seem to enjoy that cake?" the Professor remarked.

"Doos that mean 'munch'?" Bruno whispered to Sylvie.

Sylvie nodded. "It means 'to munch' and 'to *like* to munch.'"

Bruno smiled at the Professor. "I *doos* enjoy it," he said.

The Other Professor caught the word. "And I hope you're enjoying *yourself*, little Man?" he enquired.

Bruno's look of horror quite startled him. "No, *indeed* I aren't!" he said.

The Other Professor looked thoroughly puzzled. "Well, well!" he said. "Try some cowslip wine!" And he filled a glass and handed it to Bruno. "Drink this, my dear, and you'll be quite another man!"

"Who shall I be?" said Bruno, pausing in the act of putting it to his lips.

"Don't ask so many questions!" Sylvie interposed, anxious to save the poor old man from further bewilderment. "Suppose we get the Professor to tell us a story."

Bruno adopted the idea with enthusiasm. "*Please* do!" he cried eagerly. "Sumfin about tigers—and bumble-bees—and robin-redbreasts, oo knows!"

"Why should you always have *live* things in stories?" said the Professor. "Why don't you have events, or circumstances?"

"Oh, *please* invent a story like that!" cried Bruno.

The Professor began fluently enough. "Once a coincidence was taking a walk with a little accident, and they met an explanation—a *very* old explanation—so old that it was quite doubled up, and looked more like a conundrum——" he broke off suddenly.

"*Please* go on!" both children exclaimed.

The Professor made a candid confession. "It's a very difficult sort to invent, I find. Suppose Bruno tells one, first."

Bruno was only too happy to adopt the suggestion.

"Once there were a Pig, and a Accordion, and two Jars of Orange-marmalade——"

"The *dramatis personæ*," murmured the Professor. "Well, what then?"

"So, when the Pig played on the Accordion," Bruno went on, "one of the Jars of Orange-marmalade didn't like the tune, and the other Jar of Orange-marmalade did like the tune—I *know* I shall get confused among those Jars of Orange-marmalade, Sylvie!" he whispered anxiously.

"I will now recite the other Introductory Verses," said the Other Professor.

Little Birds are choking
Baronets with bun,
Taught to fire a gun:
Taught, I say, to splinter
Salmon in the winter—
Merely for the fun.

Little Birds are hiding
Crimes in carpet-bags,
Blessed by happy stags:
Blessed, I say, though beaten—
Since our friends are eaten
When the memory flags.

Little Birds are tasting
Gratitude and gold,
Pale with sudden cold:
Pale, I say, and wrinkled—
When the bells have tinkled,
And the Tale is told.

But everybody had forgotten Prince Uggug!

"He was told of the Banquet, of course?" said the Emperor.

"Undoubtedly!" replied the Professor. "*That* would be the duty of the Gold Stick in Waiting."

"Let the Gold Stick come forwards!" the Emperor gravely said.

The Gold Stick came forwards. "I attended on His Imperial Fatness," was the statement made by the trembling official. "I told him of the Lecture and the Banquet——"

"What followed?" said the Emperor: for the unhappy man seemed almost too frightened to go on.

"His Imperial Fatness was graciously pleased to be sulky. His Imperial Fatness was graciously pleased to box my ears. His Imperial Fatness was graciously pleased to say 'I don't care!'"

"'Don't-care' came to a bad end," Sylvie whispered to Bruno. "I'm not sure, but I *believe* he was hanged."

The Professor overheard her. "*That* result,"

he blandly remarked, "was merely a case of mistaken identity."

Both children looked puzzled.

"Permit me to explain. 'Don't-care' and 'Care' were twin-brothers. 'Care,' you know, killed the Cat. And they caught 'Don't-care' by mistake, and hanged him instead. And so 'Care' is alive still. But he's very unhappy without his brother. That's why they say 'Begone, dull Care!'"

"Thank you!" Sylvie said, heartily. "It's very extremely interesting. Why, it seems to explain *everything!*"

"Well, not quite *everything*," the Professor modestly rejoined. "There are two or three scientific difficulties——"

CHAPTER XXVII

THE PORCUPINE

"WHAT was your general impression as to His Imperial Fatness?" the Emperor asked the Gold Stick.

"My impression was that His Imperial Fatness was getting more——"

"More *what?*"

All listened breathlessly for the next word.

"More PRICKLY!"

"He must be sent for *at once!*" the Emperor exclaimed. And the Gold Stick went off like a shot.

Pale, trembling, speechless, the Gold Stick came slowly back again.

"Well?" said the Emperor. "Why does not the Prince appear?"

"One can easily guess," said the Professor. "His Imperial Fatness is, without doubt, a little preoccupied."

Bruno turned a look of solemn enquiry on his old friend. "What do that word mean?"

But the Professor took no notice of the question. He was eagerly listening to the Gold Stick's reply.

"Please your Highness! His Imperial Fatness is——" Not a word more could he utter.

The Empress rose in an agony of alarm. "Let us go to him!" she cried. And there was a general rush for the door.

Bruno slipped off his chair in a moment. "May we go too?" he eagerly asked. But the Emperor did not hear the question, as the Professor was speaking to him. "*Preoccupied*, your Majesty!" he was saying. "That is what he is, no doubt!"

"May we go and see him?" Bruno repeated. The Emperor nodded assent, and the children ran off. In a minute or two they returned, slowly and gravely. "Well?" said the

Emperor. "What's the matter with the Prince?"

"He's—what *you* said," Bruno replied, looking at the Professor. "That hard word." And he looked to Sylvie for assistance.

"Porcupine," said Sylvie.

And a general chorus of voices answered her. "Porcupine! Prince Uggug has turned into a Porcupine!"

"A new Specimen!" exclaimed the delighted Professor. "Pray let me go in. It should be labelled at once!"

But the strong men only pushed him back. "Label it, indeed! Do you want to be eaten up?" they cried.

"Never mind about Specimens, Professor!" said the Emperor, pushing his way through the crowd. "Tell us how to keep him safe!"

"A large cage!" the Professor promptly replied. "Bring a large cage," he said to the people generally, "with strong bars of steel, and a portcullis made to go up and down like a mouse-trap! Does any one happen to have such a thing about him?"

It didn't sound a likely sort of thing for any

one to have about him; however, they brought him one directly: curiously enough, there happened to be one standing in the gallery.

"Put it facing the opening of the door, and draw up the portcullis!" This was done in a moment.

"Blankets now!" cried the Professor. "This is a most interesting Experiment!"

There happened to be a pile of blankets close by: and the Professor had hardly said the word, when they were all unfolded and held up like curtains all around. The Professor rapidly arranged them in two rows, so as to make a dark passage, leading straight from the door to the mouth of the cage.

"Now fling the door open!" This did not need to be done: the three men had only to leap out of the way, and the fearful monster flung the door open for itself, and, with a yell like the whistle of a steam-engine, rushed into the cage.

"Down with the portcullis!" No sooner said than done: and all breathed freely once more, on seeing the Porcupine safely caged.

The Professor rubbed his hands in childish

delight. "The Experiment has succeeded!" he proclaimed. "All that is needed now is to feed it three times a day, on chopped carrots and——"

"Never mind about its food just now!" the Emperor interrupted. "Let us return to the Banquet."

"He *is* prickly, certainly," said the Professor, "but we must remember that, however porcupiny, he is royal still! After this feast is over, I'm going to take a little present to Prince Uggug—just to soothe him, you know: it isn't pleasant living in a cage."

"What'll you give him for a birthday-present?" Bruno enquired.

"A small saucer of chopped carrots," replied the Professor. "In giving birthday-presents, *my* motto is—cheapness! I should think I save forty pounds a year by giving—oh, *what* a twinge of pain!"

CHAPTER XXVIII

AFTERWARDS

"WHAT is it?" said Sylvie anxiously.

"My old enemy!" groaned the Professor. "Lumbago—rheumatism—that sort of thing. I think I'll go and lie down a bit." And he hobbled out of the Saloon, watched by the pitying eyes of the two children, whom the Empress found rather sad company. They could talk of nothing but "the dear Professor," and "what a pity he's so ill!", till at last she made the welcome proposal "Let's go and see him!"

The children eagerly grasped the hands she offered them: and we went off to the Professor's study, and found him lying on the sofa, covered up with blankets, and reading a little book.

"And how are you now, Professor?" the Empress asked, bending over the invalid.

The Professor looked up, and smiled feebly. "As devoted to your Imperial Highness as ever!" he said in a weak voice. "All of me, that is not Lumbago, is Loyalty!"

"We must take you to stay at the seaside," Sylvie said, tenderly. "It'll do you ever so much good! And the Sea's so grand!"

"But a Mountain's grander!" said Bruno.

"What is there grand about the Sea?" said the Professor. "Why, you could put it all into a teacup!"

"*Some* of it," Sylvie corrected him.

"Well, you'd only want a certain number of tea-cups to hold it *all.* And *then* where's the grandeur? Then as to a Mountain—why, you could carry it all away in a wheel-barrow, in a certain number of years!"

"It wouldn't look grand—the bits of it in the wheel-barrow," Sylvie candidly admitted.

"But when oo put it together again——" Bruno began.

"When you're older," said the Professor, "you'll know that you *ca'n't* put Mountains together again so easily! One lives and one learns, you know!"

"But it needn't be the *same* one, need it?" said Bruno. "Wo'n't it do, if *I* live, and if *Sylvie* learns?"

"I *ca'n't* learn without living!" said Sylvie.

"But I *can* live without learning!" Bruno retorted. "Oo just try me!"

"What I meant, was—" the Professor began, looking much puzzled, "—was—that you don't know *everything*, you know."

"But I *do* know everything I know!" persisted the little fellow. "I know ever so many things! Everything, 'cept the things I *don't* know. And Sylvie knows all the rest."

The Professor sighed, and gave it up. "Do you know what a Boojum is?"

"*I* know!" cried Bruno. "It's the thing what wrenches people out of their boots!"

"He means 'bootjack,'" Sylvie explained in a whisper.

"You ca'n't wrench people out of *boots*," the Professor mildly observed.

Bruno laughed saucily. "Oo *can*, though! Unless they're *welly* tight in."

"Once upon a time there was a Boojum—" the Professor began, but stopped suddenly. "I forget the rest of the Fable," he said. "And there was a lesson to be learned from it. I'm afraid I forget *that*, too."

"*I'll* tell oo a Fable!" Bruno began in a great hurry. "Once there were a Locust, and a Magpie, and a Engine-driver. And the Lesson is, to learn to get up early——"

"It isn't a bit interesting!" Sylvie said contemptuously. "You shouldn't put the Lesson so soon."

"When did you invent that Fable?" said the Professor. "Last week?"

"No!" said Bruno. "A deal shorter ago than that. Guess again!"

"I ca'n't guess," said the Professor. "How long ago?"

"Why, it isn't invented yet!" Bruno exclaimed triumphantly. "But I *have* invented a lovely one! Shall I say it?"

"If you've *finished* inventing it," said Sylvie. "And let the Lesson be 'to try again'!"

"No," said Bruno with great decision. "The

Lesson are '*not* to try again'!" "Once there were a lovely china man, what stood on the chimbley-piece. And he stood, and he stood. And one day he tumbleded off, and he didn't hurt his self one bit. Only he *would* try again. And the next time he tumbleded off, he hurted his self welly much, and breaked off ever so much varnish."

"But how did he come back on the chimney-piece after his first tumble?" said the Professor.

"*I* put him there!" cried Bruno.

"Then I'm afraid you know something about his tumbling," said the Professor. "Perhaps you pushed him?"

To which Bruno replied, very seriously, "Didn't pushed him *much*—he were a *lovely* china man," he added hastily, evidently very anxious to change the subject.

"Good night, little ones!" said the Professor. "You may leave me now—to ruminate. I'm as jolly as the day is long, except when it's necessary to ruminate on some very difficult subject. All of me," he murmured sleepily as we left the room, "all of me that isn't *Bonhommie*, is Rumination!"

"*What* did he say, Bruno?" Sylvie enquired, as soon as we were safely out of hearing.

"I *think* he said 'All of me that isn't Bone-disease is Rheumatism.'

"But oh, Sylvie, what makes the sky such a *darling* blue?"

Sylvie's sweet lips shaped themselves to reply, but her voice sounded faint and very far away. The vision was fast slipping from my eager gaze: but it seemed to me, in that last

bewildering moment, that not Sylvie but an angel was looking out through those trustful brown eyes, and that not Sylvie's but an angel's voice was whispering

"It is Love."

THE END.